A First Dictionary

For Brad, Sherry, Mark, Debby, Adam, Craig, and Amy

Cover design: James Reyman
Cover Illustration: Claude Martinot

A First Dictionary

By Harriet Wittels and Joan Greisman
Drawings by Gene Biggs

A GOLDEN BOOK ❖ NEW YORK
Golden Books Publishing Company, Inc.
New York, New York 10106

What Is a Dictionary?

A dictionary is a book of words listed in alphabetical order. It helps us know the correct spelling, the pronunciation, and the meaning of those words. This dictionary will also show you how to use the words in a sentence.

Entry Words

The words that you look up in this book are called "entry words." They are listed in alphabetical order, in large dark print. The first two entry words in the "B's" are **baby** and **bag**:

baby (ba by) a very young child, an infant
A **baby** drinks milk from a bottle.

bag a sack to hold things in
Sometimes the supermarket gives me a paper **bag**, and other times a plastic one.

Look in the "A's." What entry word comes just before **animal**?

Look in the "C's." What entry word comes right after **cart**?

Look in the "D's." What entry word comes between **day** and **deaf**?

Alphabetical Order

Since the entry words are listed alphabetically, put these words in order:

fire

exit

ice

To find the alphabetical order of the words beginning with each letter, you will have to look at the second letter, then the third letter of that word, and so on. So, when you look up the "F's" for the word **fire**, you will have to look for "i" and "r" and "e" to find the word among all the other "F" words.

Put these words in alphabetical order:

fire

finish

fine

Syllables and Pronunciation

Sometimes, after a word is first shown, it's written again in parentheses and separated into parts or syllables. This separation helps us to pronounce the word.

> **veterinarian** (vet er i **nar** i an) an animal doctor
> We took the new puppy to the **veterinarian** to get his shots.

How many syllables are in **veterinarian**?

How many syllables are in **elevator**?

How many syllables are in **funny**?

If a word is not written in parentheses, it simply means that it has only one syllable, like **safe**, **rich**, and **eye**.

Notice that one of these syllables is printed in darker letters. It means that we stress that syllable of the word when we pronounce it.

> **enjoy** (en **joy**) to get pleasure from, to like
> Did you **enjoy** your vacation at the beach?

Which syllable should you stress in the word **enjoy**?

> **motorcycle** (**mo** tor cy cle) a heavy bike run by a motor
> Even as a passenger on his **motorcycle**, I had to wear a helmet.

Which syllable should you stress in the word **motorcycle**?

Definitions

Most important of all, the dictionary gives us the meanings, or definitions, of words.

> **above** (a **bove**) over, higher than
> The third floor is **above** the second.

> **leash** a strap or chain for a pet
> Pull on his **leash** if you want him to stop.

What is the definition of the word **leash**?

Now look up the word **queer** and find its meaning.

Look up the word **marionette** and find its meaning.

Sometimes a word has more than one meaning.

stamp 1. to pound the floor with your foot
In the parade, the marching-band members all
stamp their feet in time to the music.
2. to put postage on mail
I forgot to **stamp** the letter to Patty, so it was
returned to me.

Now let's look at this sentence:

Aunt Millie kept her **false** teeth in a glass at night.

If you look up the word **false,** you will find two meanings:

1. not true, incorrect

2. fake

Which meaning tells us about Aunt Millie's teeth?

Sometimes two entry words are spelled exactly the same but are pronounced differently and have different meanings. There are numbers in front of these words in our dictionary.

1. **close** to shut
Close the door quickly, so that the dog won't
run out.

2. **close** near
Don't sit so **close** to Peter, or you'll catch his cold.

8

The word **bow** is also entered twice, with numbers in front of the word. Which number entry word fits in this sentence?

The actor took a **bow** at the end of the play.

Look it up!

That's how *A First Dictionary* works. It's easy and fun. Make using it a habit, and you'll find that it will help to improve your reading, your writing, and your speech.

Aa

abandon (a **ban** don) to leave forever, to desert
The sailors will **abandon** the ship if it starts to sink.

ability (a **bil** i ty) a skill, talent, know-how
A clown has the **ability** to make us laugh.

able (**a** ble) having skill, talent, know-how
A clown is **able** to make us laugh.

about (a **bout**) 1. around, approximately
I am **about** five feet tall.
2. concerning
I saw a science show **about** dinosaurs.

above (a **bove**) over, higher than
The third floor is **above** the second floor.

absent (**ab** sent) away, not present
Our teacher was **absent** from school yesterday.

abuse (a **buse**) to mistreat, to damage
You **abuse** your dog when you leave it locked up in a hot car.

accept (ac **cept**) to take something when offered
Please **accept** the package for me.

accident (**ac** ci dent) something that happens that is not planned or expected

He broke his leg when he had a skiing **accident.**

accomplish (ac **com** plish) to complete, to finish, to carry out

Did you **accomplish** all the tasks that I gave you?

accuse (ac **cuse**) to blame for doing wrong

He had no reason to **accuse** her of stealing his money.

ache a steady dull pain

I have an **ache** in my arm from pitching all of yesterday's game.

acrobat (**ac** ro bat) a person who can tumble, walk on a tightrope, or swing on a trapeze

The best performer in the circus was the **acrobat.**

across (a **cross**) from one side to the other

We flew **across** the Atlantic Ocean in a jet plane.

act 1. to behave

Don't **act** like a baby.

2. to perform

Are you going to **act** in the school play?

active (**ac** tive) lively, busy

Though he is old, my grandfather is still very **active.**

actor (**ac** tor) someone who performs or takes part in a play or a movie

After the show, I waited for the **actor** to give me his autograph.

add to put together

If you **add** two and two, you get four.

$$\begin{array}{r} 2 \\ + 2 \\ \hline 4 \end{array}$$

addict (**ad** dict) someone in the habit of using harmful drugs

After he became an **addict**, he started selling drugs to pay for his habit.

address (**ad** dress) exactly where a place is

The **address** of the White House is 1600 Pennsylvania Avenue, Washington, D.C.

adjust (ad **just**) to change something in order to improve it

Please **adjust** the TV to make the picture clearer.

admire (ad **mire**) to like or respect

Little boys often **admire** their big brothers.

admit (ad **mit**) 1. to confess that something is true

Did he finally **admit** that he copied his friend's homework?

2. to let in, to allow to enter

That ticket will **admit** you to the movie.

adopt (a **dopt**) to take as your own
When a man and a woman can't have a child, they sometimes **adopt** one.

adore (a **dore**) to love, to idolize
They must really **adore** that rock group if they stand in line all night for tickets.

adult (a **dult**) grown-up
On class trips we need one **adult** for every ten children.

advantage (ad **van** tage) something good that gives you an edge over others
He had the **advantage** of speaking Spanish at home before studying it in school.

adventure (ad **ven** ture) an exciting experience
The first astronauts to walk in space had the greatest **adventure** of all.

advice (ad **vice**) a suggestion about what to do
The coach gave us all **advice** on how to improve our hitting.

afford (af **ford**) to be able to pay for
We can't **afford** to go away on vacation this year.

afraid (a **fraid**) frightened, scared
Are you **afraid** of monster movies?

again (a **gain**) once more, another time
I loved Disneyland, so I'm going there **again** this summer.

age 1. the number of years old
   At what **age** can you join the Boy Scouts?
   2. a time period
   It's exciting to be living in the **age** of space travel.

agree (a **gree**) to think alike
My brother and I **agree** that orange soda is the best kind.

aim 1. to point an object toward something
   If you **aim** well, you can get the ball in the basket.
   2. a goal
   Angie's **aim** was to become a nurse.

airplane (**air** plane) a machine with wings that can
fly through the air
It took us a whole day to drive to Florida, but only two hours to
return by **airplane**.

airport (**air** port) a place where airplanes can take
off or land
We always like to get to the **airport** one hour before our
departure time.

aisle a narrow path between rows of shelves or seats
The usher walked down the **aisle** ahead of us, using his
flashlight to guide us to our row.

alarm (a **larm**) a warning signal
When they saw smoke, they rang the fire **alarm** at the corner.

album (**al** bum) a book to collect things in
We have a photo **album** for our family pictures.

alibi (**al** i bi) a reason that proves your innocence, an excuse
The man's **alibi** was that he was out of town on the night of the crime.

alien (**a** li en) a person or a creature from another land or world
E.T. was the most famous and well-liked **alien** ever in the movies.

alike (a **like**) very much the same
Amy and her mother look **alike**.

alive (a **live**) living, not dead
My grandfather died last year, but my grandmother is **alive**.

alligator (**al** li ga tor) an animal in the reptile family
An **alligator** looks a lot like a crocodile, but it has a wide, round snout and only lives in fresh water in the deep South in the United States.

allow (al **low**) to let, to permit
My parents don't **allow** me to watch TV after nine o'clock.

allowance (al **low** ance) a set amount of spending money
Every Friday Dad gives me my weekly **allowance**.

almost (**al** most) nearly
Mark is **almost** as tall as his brother Brad.

alone (a **lone**) by oneself
My grandmother lives **alone**, but she spends the holidays with us.

alphabet (**al** pha bet) a set of letters that make up all the words of a language
My little sister learned the **alphabet** from A to Z by watching *Sesame Street*.

also (**al** so) too, in addition
John gets good grades in science, math, and **also** social studies.

always (**al** ways) 1. every time
I **always** get to school by eight o'clock.
2. forever, for keeps
I hope you will **always** be my best friend.

amateur (**am** a teur) one who does an activity for fun rather than money, a beginner at some activity
Adam is an **amateur** basketball player.

amaze (a **maze**) to surprise, to astound
The speed of that little boat will **amaze** you.

ambulance (**am** bu lance) a special car or van that is used to carry sick or injured people to a hospital
The police called an **ambulance** to the scene of the accident.

amuse (a **muse**) to entertain, to make laugh
A comic book can **amuse** us on a rainy day.

angry (**an** gry) furious, enraged
The dog gets **angry** when we tease him.

animal (**an** i mal) a living thing that is not a plant
My cat is my favorite **animal**.

anniversary (an ni **ver** sa ry) the return each year of some special date
My parents celebrate their wedding **anniversary** each year on June 9.

announce (an **nounce**) to make known to everyone
The principal will **announce** the name of the essay-contest winner over the loudspeaker.

annoy (an **noy**) to bother, to disturb, to pester
Don't **annoy** him while he's studying.

answer (**an** swer) a reply
Sherry was the only one who knew the right **answer** to that hard question.

apartment (a **part** ment) a set of rooms in a building to live in
My family just moved into a four-room **apartment**.

apologize (a **pol** o gize) to say you are sorry
I was wrong and I **apologize** for not inviting you to my birthday party.

appear (ap **pear**) to be seen, to arrive
The team had to **appear** before the game could begin.

appetite (**ap** pe tite) a hunger for food
He has a good **appetite** except when he is sick with the flu.

applaud (ap **plaud**) to clap your hands to show that you like something
We started to **applaud** as soon as the actors came onstage.

appointment (ap **point** ment) an agreement to be somewhere at a particular time, a date
She was late for her **appointment** at the dentist's office.

appreciate (ap **pre** ci ate) to see the value of
The teacher took us to museums so that we could **appreciate** the work of famous artists.

approve (ap **prove**) to say yes to
My parents **approve** of studying on school nights.

April (**A** pril) the fourth month of the year
April showers bring May flowers.

aquarium (a **quar** i um) a fish tank
We bought goldfish and water plants and put them into our classroom **aquarium**.

area (**ar** e a) a section, a location
There's an **area** in our schoolyard just for playing basketball.

argue (**ar** gue) to disagree, to quarrel

Brothers and sisters sometimes **argue** about which TV channel to watch.

arithmetic (a **rith** me tic) the study of the use of numbers

The rules of **arithmetic** tell us how to multiply and divide.

army (**ar** my) a country's soldiers, troops

My uncle joined the **army** so he could help fight the war.

arrange (ar **range**) to put in order, to organize

I'm going to **arrange** my looseleaf book according to subjects.

arrest (ar **rest**) to capture a person and put him in jail

The police had to **arrest** the bank robber, because he had committed a crime.

arrive (ar **rive**) to come, to get to

When did you **arrive** at the train station?

article (**ar** ti cle) a written news item

We each had to bring in an **article** from yesterday's newspaper to discuss in Current Events.

artificial (ar ti **fi** cial) not real, imitating something natural

She almost watered an **artificial** plant that looked just like a real one.

artist (**ar** tist) a person who paints or draws pictures
Only an outstanding **artist** has his work shown in a museum.

ashamed (a **shamed**) embarrassed, feeling sorry
and guilty
I was **ashamed** because I lied to my best friend.

ask to question
We'll have to **ask** for directions before we drive to the beach.

asleep (a **sleep**) not awake
Sometimes you dream when you are **asleep**.

assembly (as **sem** bly) a group of people gathered
together
Every Wednesday we have an **assembly** of the third grade.

assignment (as **sign** ment) a job or task given to a
certain person or group
Our homework **assignment** last night was to study for the
spelling test.

assist (as **sist**) to help
The scout leader said he would **assist** us in setting up our
tents.

astronaut (**as** tro naut) a person who travels in
space
Neil Armstrong was the first **astronaut** to walk on the moon.

athlete (**ath** lete) a person with ability in one or more sports

Tommy was such a good **athlete** that he pitched and batted cleanup on the baseball team.

atlas (**at** las) a book of maps

We studied the geography of the United States in the **atlas**.

attach (at **tach**) to connect, to join

I'll **attach** the teacher's note to my homework papers.

attack (at **tack**) to charge suddenly

The enemy would always **attack** after dark.

attention (at **ten** tion) careful listening, concentration

The lion tamer had the animals' **attention**, and all of ours.

attitude (**at** ti tude) a feeling about something

I don't like your grouchy **attitude** whenever you lose a game.

attract (at **tract**) to pull, to draw

I used my magnet to **attract** the safety pins that had fallen to the floor.

audience (**au** di ence) a group of people watching or listening to a performance

The **audience** clapped at the end of the play.

auditorium (aù di **tor** i um) a large room where people watch a performance

The sixth graders put on *The Wizard of Oz* in our school **auditorium**.

August (**Au** gust) the eighth month of the year

In **August**, we spend our time in the pool;
on a very hot day, that's the way to keep cool.

aunt the sister of your father or your mother

My **aunt** has three children who are my cousins.

author (**au** thor) the writer of a work

Robert Louis Stevenson is the **author** of *Treasure Island*.

autobiography (au to bi **og** ra phy) the story of a person's life, written by that same person

The teacher asked each of us to write his or her **autobiography**.

autograph (**au** to graph) a person's name signed in his own handwriting

Craig traded Doc Gooden's **autograph** for Don Mattingly's.

automatic (au to **mat** ic) working by itself

We have an **automatic** garage door that Dad can open by remote control while we're still in the car.

automobile (au to mo **bile**) a car

The Ford Model T was a famous **automobile.**

autumn (**au** tumn) the season of the year between summer and winter

.In **autumn**, the leaves change color and fall off the trees.

avoid (a **void**) to stay away from

I **avoid** woolly sweaters that make me itch.

award (a **ward**) a prize, a reward

In Hollywood each year, they give an **award** to the best actor.

awful (**aw** ful) terrible, dreadful

The weather was so **awful** that our plane took off an hour late.

Bb

baby (**ba** by) a very young child, an infant
A **baby** drinks milk from a bottle.

bag a sack
Sometimes the supermarket gives me a paper **bag,** and other times a plastic one.

bagel (**ba** gel) a chewy roll with a hole in the middle
On Sunday mornings, I always eat a **bagel** with cream cheese.

baggage (**bag** gage) suitcases, luggage
The bellhop carried all our **baggage** into the hotel.

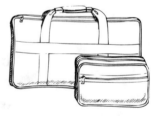

bake to cook in an oven
My grandmother can **bake** the best chocolate-chip cookies.

bald without hair
My grandfather has a shiny **bald** head.

ball a round toy
He bounced the **ball** on the sidewalk.

balloon (bal **loon**) a rubber bag filled with air or gas
When he let go of the string, the **balloon** flew away.

band a group of people who play music together
Jeff plays the drums in the school **band**.

bank a safe place to keep money
My parents opened a savings account for me in a **bank** on Main Street.

barber (**bar** ber) a person who cuts hair
I told the **barber** not to cut my hair too short.

bark 1. the sound a dog makes
Sometimes even a poodle's **bark** is loud and scary.
2. the hard outer skin of a tree
The oak's **bark** protects it from harm.

barn a farm building where equipment and animals are kept
The cows went into the **barn** to eat and to sleep.

baseball (**base** ball) a sport played with a bat and a ball and fielding mitts by two teams of nine players each on a field with four bases
In a game of **baseball,** a pitcher and his fielders try to prevent the batting team from getting hits and scoring runs by rounding the bases.

basement (**base** ment) the lowest floor of a building
We have our washing machine down in the **basement**.

basket (**bas** ket) a container made of wood or straw
We keep our dirty laundry in a big covered **basket**.

basketball (**bas** ket ball) a sport played with a large ball by two teams of five players each on a court with raised baskets and a backboard at each end

In a game of **basketball,** the teams run back and forth, each trying to score points against the other team by shooting the ball into the opposing team's basket.

bat 1. a wooden or metal stick used to hit a ball

Every baseball player likes to use his own lucky **bat.**

2. a mouselike animal with wings

A **bat** sleeps during the day and flies around at night.

bath a washing of the body in a tub of water

The baby gets a **bath** every night after supper.

battery (**bat** ter y) a cell that provides electric power

I need one square **battery** to make my radio work.

battle (**bat** tle) a fight, a struggle

The two gangs had a terrible **battle** out in the street.

bazaar (ba **zaar**) a market where things are sold, sometimes to raise money for a cause

At the last church **bazaar,** we raised money for a summer-camp program.

beach an area, usually covered with sand, at the edge of an ocean or a lake

I love to go to the **beach** and walk on the warm sand.

bear a kind of large, strong, furry animal
The polar **bear** has white fur and lives way up north, where it is very cold.

beard the hair on a man's face
Pictures of Santa Claus always show him with a long white **beard**.

beat 1. to hit, to strike
When no one answered his knock, the man **beat** on the door with his fists.
2. to win over, to defeat
We were happy to **beat** the other team today.
3. to mix fast
The baker had to **beat** four eggs as part of the recipe for cupcakes.

beautiful (**beau** ti ful) very pretty, lovely to look at
Wasn't the bride **beautiful** in her wedding dress?

bed a piece of furniture used for sleeping
I sleep in a **bed** now, but the baby sleeps in a crib.

bee a kind of flying insect that can sting
A **bee** makes honey and helps flowers grow.

beg to ask again and again
I had to **beg** him to let me ride his new bike.

begin (be **gin**) to start
To **begin** the game, you have to shuffle the cards and deal five cards to each player.

behave (be **have**) to act in a certain way

We sent our dog to a training school, so that he would learn how to **behave** properly.

believe (be **lieve**)   1. to think, to suppose

I **believe** that it's his turn up at bat.

2. to trust, to accept as true

Do you **believe** that there are such things as ghosts?

belt a piece of clothing that is worn around the waist

He wore a cowboy **belt** with a horseshoe buckle.

bench a long seat

The men who were not in the game sat and waited on the **bench**.

bicycle (**bi** cy cle) a two-wheeler

John's legs were very tired from pedaling his **bicycle** around the lake.

big   1. large

The **big** cage has enough room for two parrots.

2. important

Little League is having a **big** game this weekend.

bill 1. a piece of paper that tells an amount of money owed

The gas and electric **bill** arrived in the mail today.

2. paper money

Mary paid me back with a five-dollar **bill**.

3. a bird's beak

The pigeon picked up the bread crumbs with its **bill**.

biography (bi **og** ra phy) the story of a person's life

The **biography** of Abraham Lincoln begins with his life in a log cabin.

bird an animal with feathers and wings

The **bird** laid its eggs in a nest near my window.

birth the beginning of life

When we were at the aquarium, we saw the **birth** of a baby whale.

birthday (**birth** day) the day someone is born, the anniversary of that day

Richard has a party in school every year on his **birthday**.

bite to grip or tear with the teeth

If you tease that dog, it might **bite** you!

blade the sharp part of a tool that cuts

My father changes the **blade** in his razor whenever it gets dull.

blame to accuse
Blame someone for taking your money only if you're very sure that person took it.

blanket (**blank** et) a covering
I kick the **blanket** off my bed if I get hot during the night.

bleed to lose blood
Did your knee **bleed** when you scraped it?

blind not able to see
The **blind** man used a cane to help him walk down the street.

blizzard (**bliz** zard) a heavy snowstorm with strong winds
Our school was closed for two days during last winter's **blizzard**.

block 1. a toy that is a small cube of wood
The baby stacked one **block** on another till she had built a tall tower.
2. a section of a city street
The bus stops at every other **block**.

board a long piece of wood
We went to the lumberyard to buy a new **board** for our fence.

boast to show off, to brag
Robert was always ready to **boast** about his bowling scores.

boat a craft that carries people on the water
She rowed the **boat** across the lake.

bomb a weapon that can explode
The spy put a **bomb** under the desk.

bone a hard part inside the body that helps make up the skeleton
He broke a **bone** in his leg when he had a skiing accident.

book a set of pages held together between two covers
This dictionary is a **book** of words for young children.

boot a high shoe made of leather or rubber
The toe on a cowboy **boot** comes to a point.

border (**bor** der)   1. an edge, a rim
   I painted a **border** around my picture.
   2. the line between two countries or states
   We drove across the **border** from the United States to Mexico.

boring (**bor** ing) dull, uninteresting
The movie was so **boring** that I fell asleep.

born brought into the world
My baby brother was **born** six months ago.

borrow (**bor** row) to take for a time something you will return

If you have a library card, you can **borrow** books from the library.

boss someone in charge

The **boss** told the workers to clean up the mess.

bother (**both** er) to give trouble to, to annoy

Don't **bother** me when I'm doing my homework.

bottle (**bot** tle) a container made of glass or plastic that holds liquids

I like to drink my soda right out of the **bottle**.

bottom (**bot** tom) the lowest part

Our instructor gave us our first ski lesson at the **bottom** of the hill.

bounce to spring back up when thrown down

The basketball player saw the ball **bounce** out of the court.

boundary (**bound** a ry) the dividing line between two places

Sometimes mountains form a **boundary** between two states.

1. bow to bend the body and head forward

The actor took a **bow** at the end of the play.

2. bow 1. a tie with loops

She wears a **bow** in her hair.

2. a curved weapon for shooting arrows

Ages ago, a hunter would use a **bow** and arrow to kill animals.

3. a thin stick used to play a violin or other instrument

She put the violin under her chin and took the **bow** in her hand.

bowl a deep round dish

We always eat soup from a **bowl**.

1. box a container for holding or storing things, a crate

I bought a small **box** of popcorn at the movies.

2. box to fight with the fists

They put on their gloves, the bell rang, and they started to **box**.

bracelet (**brace** let) a piece of jewelry worn around the wrist

She got a gold **bracelet** for her birthday.

braces (**bra** ces) wires and bands used to straighten the teeth

The dentist told Jackie that she would need to wear **braces** for two years.

brag to show off, to boast

Other people hate to hear you **brag** about yourself.

brake the part of a moving machine that slows it down or stops it
  I keep my foot on the **brake** of my bike when I go downhill.

branch an arm of a tree that sticks out from the trunk
  The monkey was swinging from one large **branch** to another.

brand a particular kind of some product
  What **brand** of cereal do you like?

brat a spoiled or nasty child
  He behaved like a **brat** in the toy store.

brave having courage, without fear
  Police officers and fire fighters are very **brave** men and women.

1. break to crack, to split, to shatter
  That glass will **break** if you drop it.

2. break a rest or a recess
  We had a spring **break** from school at Easter time.

breakfast (**break** fast) the first meal of the day
  I usually have orange juice, cereal, and milk for **breakfast**.

breathe to take air into the lungs and let it out again
  You **breathe** very hard after you run.

brick a block of clay that has been baked to make it hard, used in building

One of the three little pigs placed one **brick** atop another to build his house.

bride a woman about to be or just married

The **bride** wore a white gown.

bridge an overpass that lets people cross from one side of an obstacle to the other

We had to drive over the **bridge** to get across the river.

bright 1. shiny, giving much light

Everyone wore dark glasses to protect their eyes from the **bright** sun.

2. smart, clever

She was so **bright** that they had to put her in a special advanced class.

bring to take along, to carry

We all **bring** our lunch when we go on a class trip.

broom a brush with a long handle, used for sweeping

When the handle of the **broom** broke off, they used it for playing stickball.

brother (**broth** er) a boy or man with the same parents as another person

Tom has one **brother** in his family.

bucket (**buck** et) a pail, an open container with a handle that is used for carrying things

The farmer filled a **bucket** with water and took it to his house.

buddy (**bud** dy) a close friend, a partner
On camping trips, each of us always hikes with a **buddy** so no one will get lost.

build to make, to put together
Babies like to **build** things with blocks and then knock them down.

bump 1. the banging together of two things
      We felt a **bump** behind us and later found a dent where the other car had hit ours.
    2. a swelling, a lump
      The baby fell down and got a **bump** on his head.

bunch a group of things that are alike
I ate a whole **bunch** of grapes at the beach.

bundle (**bun** dle) a package
We gave away a big **bundle** of used clothing for the poor.

burglar (**bur** glar) someone who breaks into a house to steal, a robber
The police caught the **burglar** as he climbed out a window with the TV set.

burn to be on fire, to set on fire
If the fire fighters do not spray the flaming house, it will **burn** to the ground.

bury (**bur** y) to put into the ground and cover
I felt so sad when my pet hamster died and I had to **bury** him.

bus a long kind of van with seats for many riders
A school **bus** picks up the kids who live far away and takes them to school.

business (**busi** ness) a company that buys and sells goods or services
My uncle is in the **business** of selling sneakers and sweatsuits.

busy (**bus** y) active, having a lot to do
With school, piano lessons, and Little League, he is as **busy** as can be.

button (**but** ton) a kind of fastener sewn on a piece of clothing to keep it closed
I always keep the top **button** of my shirt open.

buy to get something by paying for it
I'm saving my money to **buy** a new bike.

Cc

cabin (**cab** in) 1. a simply built house, usually made of wood

Abraham Lincoln was born in a log **cabin**.

2. a room on a ship

Our **cabin** was on the main deck, near the swimming pool.

cable (**ca** ble) a bundle of wires that carry electricity

We are able to see more TV stations because our set was plugged to a special **cable**.

cactus (**cac** tus) a kind of plant with spines that grows in hot, dry places

Some types of desert **cactus** grow taller than a person.

cafeteria (caf e **te** ri a) a self-service restaurant

In our school **cafeteria,** we clear the tables ourselves.

cage a box with metal or wooden bars that houses animals or birds

When I opened the **cage,** the canary flew out.

cake a dessert made from sweet batter and baked in an oven

Everyone had a slice of chocolate **cake** after dinner.

calculator (**cal** cu la tor) a machine that does mathematical problems

I can do my arithmetic homework much faster if I use a **calculator**.

calendar (**cal** en dar) a chart showing the months, weeks, and days of the year

A **calendar** usually shows all the holidays of every season.

call 1. to telephone

Don't forget to **call** if you're going to be late.

2. to cry out

Call out the answer as soon as you think you have it.

3. to name

What will you **call** your new kitten?

calm still, peaceful

The ocean was too **calm** for surfing.

camel (**cam** el) a kind of large, shaggy animal with humps on its back

A **camel** can go for many days without drinking water.

camera (**cam** er a) a machine that takes photographs

He looked into the **camera,** counted to three, then snapped our picture.

camp a vacation place in the country, often with lots of sports and other activities for children

At her summer **camp,** Nancy shared a cabin with seven other girls.

cancel (**can** cel) to put an end to

They had to **cancel** the picnic when it continued to rain.

candidate (**can** di date) someone who runs for office

Geraldine Ferraro was the first woman **candidate** for Vice President of the United States.

candle (**can** dle) a stick of wax with a string in the middle that is burned to give light

During the storm the lights went out, so we lit a **candle** until the electricity came back on.

candy (**can** dy) sweet snacks often mixed with chocolate, fruits, or nuts

On Halloween, people usually give out **candy** as a treat.

cane a stick to lean on that helps someone to walk

When he broke his toe, he used a **cane** to get around.

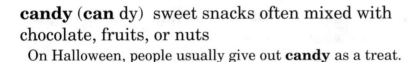

canoe (ca **noe**) a light, narrow paddle boat, pointed at both ends

When he stood up in the **canoe,** it tipped over.

cap 1. a small hat

The President put on a baseball **cap** when he threw out the first ball of the season.

2. a cover for something, a top that fits

Did you put the **cap** back on the toothpaste?

capital (**cap** i tal) the city in a state or country where the government meets

Joey has memorized every **capital** in the United States.

captain (**cap** tain) the leader of a group

The team's **captain** gave the players a pep talk before the game.

capture (**cap** ture) to catch, to trap

It took five hours for the animal trainers to **capture** the circus lion.

car an automobile, a kind of machine with an engine that goes on wheels

He doesn't like to fly, so he drove his **car** all the way.

career (ca **reer**) the work someone chooses to do, a profession

The kids in Little League dream of making baseball their **career**.

careful (**care** ful) thinking before acting, cautious

Be **careful** when you come around that sharp curve in the road.

careless (**care** less) thoughtless, sloppy

She was **careless** about putting things away, so she couldn't find things when she needed them

carnival (**car** ni val) an outdoor event with rides, games, and entertainment

I won a big stuffed animal at the **carnival**.

carpenter (**car** pen ter) a person who builds things from wood

The **carpenter** made shelves to hold all the books.

carpet (**car** pet) a rug

A **carpet** covered the whole bedroom floor.

carriage (**car** riage) 1. a wheeled cart for a baby

The parents pushed the **carriage** down the block, then folded it up and put it into the trunk of the car.

2. a large wheeled cart for people that is pulled by horses

The king and queen waved to the people from their **carriage**.

carrot (**car** rot) A long orange root that is healthy to eat

The rabbit was eating a **carrot**.

carry (**car** ry) to hold and move from one place to another

The supermarket hires boys to **carry** packages to people's cars.

cart a wagon with wheels that is used for carrying things

We always take a small **cart** to the store when we have to bring a big order home from the supermarket.

cartoon (**car** toon) a funny drawing, a short movie made of such drawings

Bugs Bunny is the star of my favorite **cartoon**.

carve to cut, to slice

It's the custom in our house to have Grandpa **carve** the turkey on Thanksgiving Day.

case a box or package that holds something

They ordered a **case** of soda for the party.

cash money in the form of coins and bills

Adults pay with checks and credit cards, but children always use **cash**.

cashier (cash **ier**) the person who takes money from customers and gives them change

Every server at McDonald's is also a **cashier.**

cast 1. the group of performers in a play

The play had a **cast** of just two people.

2. a stiff bandage

He had a **cast** on his broken leg for six weeks.

castle (**cas** tle) a strong, safe building where royalty lived

The thick stone walls of a **castle** protected the royal families from their enemies.

catch to grab hold of something

Try to **catch** the ball before it bounces.

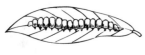

caterpillar (**cat** er pil lar) an insect that looks like a worm but changes into a moth or butterfly

The furry **caterpillar** crawled up the tree trunk to get to the tasty leaves.

cattle (**cat** tle) cows and bulls
Farmers raise **cattle** for both milk and meat.

cavity (**cav** i ty) a hole in the tooth, caused by decay
A dentist will put a filling in your **cavity**.

ceiling (**ceil** ing) the top of a room
He painted the **ceiling** with a roller on a long stick.

celebrate (**cel** e brate) to honor with joy and happiness
We always **celebrate** Mother's Day by having a party for Mom.

celebrity (ce **leb** ri ty) a famous person
People always bother a **celebrity** for his autograph.

cell a room in a jail
There was a sink, a toilet, and a bed in each **cell**.

cellar (**cel** lar) an underground room at the bottom of a building
After the last storm, we had a flood in our **cellar**.

cemetery (**cem** e ter y) a place where the dead are buried, a graveyard
We buried our dog in a pet **cemetery**.

center (**cen** ter) 1. the middle

The **center** of a doughnut is a hole.

2. a gathering place for an activity or activities

On Tuesdays, I go to an after-school **center** to take music lessons.

century (**cen** tu ry) one hundred years

It's hard to imagine what new inventions we'll see in the next **century**.

cereal (**ce** re al) a breakfast food made from grain

I like to eat my **cereal** with bananas, raisins, and milk.

chain 1. a row of metal links connected together

The light above the dining room table hung from a long **chain**.

2. a group of related things

Burger King is a **chain** of hamburger restaurants.

chair a seat with legs and a back

When I leaned back on two legs of my **chair,** I fell.

champion (**cham** pi on) someone who is the best at a game or sport

John McEnroe was a tennis **champion**.

chance 1. an opportunity

Did you have a **chance** to play your new video yet?

2. a possibility

There's a good **chance** that it will rain this afternoon.

change 1. a difference

> When he got his new eyeglasses, there was a **change** in his schoolwork.

2. a switch

> Bring a **change** of clothing if you're sleeping over.

Chanukah (**Cha** nu kah) an eight-day Jewish festival celebrated by the lighting of candles

We usually celebrate **Chanukah** in December with lots of games, presents, and good food.

charge 1. to ask a price for something

> How much did they **charge** for your sneakers?

2. to run with force

> The bull lowered his head and got ready to **charge**.

3. to accuse, to blame

> The policeman had to **charge** him with driving without a license.

4. to fill with electricity

> I need to **charge** my portable radio before I can use it again.

5. to use a credit card to make a purchase

> Mom had no cash, so she had to **charge** our meal.

chase 1. to run after

> If I throw a ball, my dog will **chase** it.

2. to drive away

> Mary always has to **chase** the cat from her room.

cheap 1. low in price

Candy bars used to be **cheap** — only twenty-five cents each!

2. not willing to spend money, stingy

He's too **cheap** to treat his friends to ice cream.

cheat to be dishonest

He wanted an "A" but he didn't know the answers, so he tried to **cheat** by keeping his book open during the test.

check to test something to see if it is as it should be

Let me **check** the tires on your bike to make sure they're not getting flat.

cheer to shout with joy, to encourage

Everyone started to **cheer** when the bases were loaded.

chew to grind with your teeth

You should **chew** very well before you swallow.

chicken (**chick** en) a kind of bird that is used for food

One type of **chicken** is raised to become food for us to eat, while another type is raised to lay eggs for us to eat.

chief the leader of a group

The fire **chief** gave orders to the fire fighters at the scene.

child a young boy or girl

A **child** cannot get into that movie without an adult.

choke to block the breathing

It's scary to have a piece of food **choke** you.

choose to pick out

The two captains were supposed to **choose** the best players for their teams.

chore a small job

It's my **chore** to dry the supper dishes.

Christmas (**Christ** mas) a holiday that celebrates the birth of Christ

Most Christians celebrate **Christmas** every year on December 25.

chunk a large piece

Mother put out a **chunk** of cheese for our company to snack on.

circus (**cir** cus) a show with acrobats, trained animals, and clowns

The **circus** comes to our town in the spring.

city (**cit** y) a large town where people live and work

We leave the **city** every summer to go on vacation in the country.

clap to applaud

If you're happy and you know it, **clap** your hands.

class a group of children in one schoolroom

Our **class** was divided into two groups for reading.

clean not dirty or soiled

It's hard to keep a shirt **clean** when you're eating pizza.

clear 1. bright and sunny

On a **clear** day, you can see all the way across the river.

2. easy to understand

Bob's report on George Washington made the life of the first President very **clear** to all of us.

climate (**cli** mate) the usual weather in a certain area

The **climate** in Puerto Rico is hot and humid.

climb to move up on

The fire fighters had to **climb** the tree to rescue the cat.

clock a machine that tells the time

If I didn't keep an eye on the clock, I'd never get to school on time.

1. close to shut

Close the door quickly so that the dog won't run out.

2. close near

If you sit **close** to Peter, you'll catch his cold.

closet (**clos** et) a small compartment with a door, where things are stored

The **closet** in the hallway is just for jackets and coats.

clothing (**cloth** ing) things that are worn

A swimsuit and flippers are all the **clothing** he has on today.

clown a circus performer who makes people laugh

The **clown** wore funny shoes that were much too big for his feet.

club 1. a stick used for hitting

A policeman always carries a **club** on his belt.

2. a group of people who meet for some reason

My father goes to a bridge **club** every Monday to play cards.

clue some proof that helps to solve a mystery, a hint

The fingerprint on the safe was the **clue** that told us who had stolen the money.

clumsy (**clum** sy) awkward when moving or handling things

The **clumsy** waiter spilled a glass of water and dropped some silverware.

coach the trainer of a team

The gym teacher was also the **coach** of the soccer team.

cold having a low temperature, chilly

The **cold** wind made it seem like the temperature was below zero.

collect (col **lect**) 1. to gather, to save

> He started to **collect** coins when his aunt brought him some francs from France.

2. to pick up

> They **collect** the garbage on our block at noon every day.

combine (com **bine**) mix, to put together

I like to **combine** sunflower seeds and raisins for an afternoon snack.

comedian (co **me** di an) a funny performer

The **comedian** told some jokes that really made us laugh.

comfortable (**com** fort a ble)

> 1. cozy

> The most **comfortable** seat in the house is the sofa.

> 2. happy, at ease

> After we moved, it took me time to feel **comfortable** in my new home.

commercial (com **mer** cial) an advertisement on TV or radio

When a **commercial** interrupts our favorite show, we all run to the kitchen for a snack.

committee (com **mit** tee) a group of people who meet to do a certain job
Parents and teachers formed a **committee** to study the drug problem.

company (**com** pa ny)   1. visitors, guests
I have to share my room when **company** stays over at our house.
2. a business
When the radio needed repair, my father sent it back to the **company** that made it.

compare (com **pare**) to study how things are the same or different
My mother sent me to **compare** the prices of two different pairs of sneakers so I could choose the less expensive one.

compass (**com** pass) a device used to show direction
The needle on a **compass** always points to the north.

complain (com **plain**) to say that something is not right or bothers you
If you think you got the wrong change in the store, **complain** to the manager.

complete (com **plete**) to finish up
Be sure to **complete** your homework before you meet your friends.

computer (com **put** er) a machine that can store information and solve problems

After I use it to do my homework, I play games with my **computer**.

concentrate (**con** cen trate) to give all your attention to something

It was hard to **concentrate** on my homework with all the noise outside.

conference (**con** fer ence) a meeting, a discussion

Every year they set one night aside for a parent-teacher **conference**.

confess (con **fess**) to tell the truth, to admit

When they caught him in the act, he had to **confess** that he did it.

confuse (con **fuse**) to mix up

Don't **confuse** the can of hair spray with the can of room freshener.

congratulate (con **grat** u late) to tell someone you share their happiness

Did the principal **congratulate** him on winning the spelling bee?

connect (con **nect**) to join, to attach

Her little sister liked to **connect** the dots to make a picture.

consent (con **sent**) permission

I need my mother's **consent** to go on the trip.

container (con **tain** er) something—like a jar or a box—that holds something else

Put the **container** of milk back in the refrigerator.

contest (con test) an activity where people compete in hopes of being judged the winner

Miss America, the most famous beauty **contest** of all, is held in Atlantic City each September.

continue (con **tin** ue) 1. to go on without stopping

Are you going to **continue** taking piano lessons till you're a grown-up?

2. to start again

We'll **continue** our game of checkers after supper.

contribute (con **trib** ute) to give, to donate

We all worked hard to **contribute** money to the Children's Hospital.

conversation (con ver **sa** tion) talk between two or more people

You must keep your **conversation** quiet in a library.

cook to prepare food, using heat

On a camping trip, it's fun to **cook** foods over a fire.

cooperate (co **op** er ate) to work or act together with others

When each of us does his chore, we **cooperate** and the job gets finished quickly.

copy (**cop** y) 1. to imitate
> Don't **copy** the silly things he does.
2. to duplicate something
> If you are absent, you'll have to **copy** the homework assignment from someone else.

corner (**cor** ner) a place where two sides meet
The **corner** of a square is called a right angle.

correct (cor **rect**) to check over and make something right
The words were put on the board so we could **correct** our own spelling tests.

cost to be priced at, to be worth
How much does that watch **cost**?

costume (**cos** tume) clothing worn by a person pretending to be someone else
I had to wear a toad **costume** for my part in *The Wind in the Willows.*

cot a narrow bed that folds up
When Tommy visited us, he slept on a **cot** in my room.

couch a sofa, a piece of furniture for two or more people to sit on
Four of us can sit comfortably on our **couch** and watch TV.

counselor (**coun** sel or) 1. an advisor

The guidance **counselor** recommended a special school for my brother.

2. a group leader

In camp last summer, one **counselor** taught everyone how to water-ski.

count 1. to add up

Count the number of people in front of us in line.

2. to say numbers in order

Can you start with fifty and **count** up to one hundred?

country (**coun** try) a nation, like the United States, where people live under one government

Our **country** is made up of people from many other countries of the world who chose to come here and be Americans.

courage (**cour** age) bravery

He showed a lot of **courage** when he parachuted from the plane.

courteous (**cour** te ous) polite, thoughtful

It is **courteous** to hold the door for a person carrying heavy packages.

cover (**cov** er) something that fits over another thing

That big lid was not the right **cover** for the small pot.

coward (**cow** ard) someone who acts afraid and timid

My dog barks at everyone, but he turns into a **coward** when a bigger dog barks at him.

cowboy (**cow** boy) a man who takes care of cattle

A **cowboy** usually gets around on horseback to tend his herd.

crack 1. a split, a break

The ball hit the window and left a **crack** in it.

2. a quick, sharp sound

The **crack** of the trainer's whip made the lions back up in the ring.

3. a dangerous drug

Kids who use **crack** ruin their lives.

crash a bad collision, with a loud noise

No passengers were hurt in the car **crash**.

crawl to move very close to the ground on your hands and knees

When the baby learned to **crawl,** we knew that soon she would start to walk.

crayon (**cray** on) a stick of colored wax used for writing or drawing

She used a black **crayon** and an orange **crayon** to color the Halloween poster.

crazy (**cra** zy) insane, mentally ill

When he started to act **crazy,** they had to put him in a special hospital.

crib a baby's bed that is closed on four sides
Mother puts down one side of the **crib** when she changes the baby's diaper.

crime an act that is against the law
Stealing is a **crime.**

crocodile (**croc** o dile) an animal in the reptile family, like an alligator
A **crocodile** has a head that is longer than an alligator's.

crook a person who is dishonest, one who steals
The **crook** picked the wallet out of the lady's purse.

crooked (**crook** ed) 1. not straight
He drew a very **crooked** line because he didn't use a ruler.
2. not honest
It was a **crooked** game, because the dealer looked at other people's cards.

crop the food a farmer grows, harvests, and sells
That farmer sold some of his corn **crop** at a roadside stand.

crowd a large group of people close together, a mob
A **crowd** gathered to watch the parade.

cruel (**cru** el) mean, unkind
It's **cruel** to make horses work when the weather is very hot or very cold.

crush to press down with force, to squash
You'll **crush** the bread if you pack it under the other groceries in the bag.

cry to make an unhappy sound, to have tears run from your eyes, to weep
I heard the baby **cry** when it was time for her bottle.

cup a short open container with a handle, used for drinking or measuring
I drank a **cup** of hot chocolate when I came off the skating rink.

cure a treatment that makes better some disease or ailment
The doctor said bed rest was the best **cure** for my cold.

curious (**cu** ri ous) wanting to learn or know
We were **curious** about the eating and sleeping habits of the seals.

customer (**cus** tom er) someone who shops for or buys something
The saleswoman tried to help the **customer** find shoes in the right size.

cut 1. to divide with a sharp edge
We used a knife to **cut** the cake into eight slices.

cut   2. to slit or slash

I **cut** my finger with the sharp knife.

3. to shorten

We **cut** our vacation by three days because the weather was so bad.

cute charming, darling

The cheerleaders are all talented and **cute**.

Dd

damage (**dam** age) to harm, to hurt
You'll **damage** your bike if you ride it down that dirt road.

dance to move in time to music
She brought records to the party so we could **dance**.

dangerous (**dan** ger ous) unsafe, able to cause harm
It is **dangerous** to ride in a car without wearing a seat belt.

dark not light, dim
In the wintertime, the days are short and the sky gets **dark** early.

date   1. one day on a calendar
Valentine's Day is always celebrated on the same **date,** February 14.
2. an appointment
We had a **date** to go bowling on Thursday night.

daughter (**daught** er) someone's child who is a girl
Helen is her parents' oldest **daughter**.

dawn the first light of the morning
The little boy got up very early to see the **dawn**.

day 1. twenty-four hours

It takes just about a **day** for the train to travel from New York to Florida.

2. the time from sunrise to sunset, the opposite of night

Tony's father sleeps during the **day** because he has a night job.

dead not alive anymore

They knew the goldfish was **dead** when they found it floating on top of the water.

deaf not able to hear

The **deaf** children were learning sign language.

December (De **cem** ber) the twelfth month of the year

'Tis the night before Christmas, **December** is here; we're all wrapping gifts for our near and our dear.

decide (de **cide**) to make up your mind

Did you **decide** to go to camp this summer?

decorate (**dec** o rate) to make attractive or pretty

We put up streamers and balloons to **decorate** the room for the party.

deep from front to back or from top to bottom

The lake was twelve feet **deep** out near the raft.

definition (def i **ni** tion) the meaning of a word
In this dictionary, the **definition** of the word *dead* is "not alive anymore."

delicatessen (del i ca **tes** sen) a kind of store that sells foods and other household supplies
We picked up sandwiches for our picnic at the corner **delicatessen**.

delicious (de **li** cious) very good to eat, tasty
There's nothing as **delicious** as warm chocolate-chip cookies.

deliver (de **liv** er) to bring and give
He has to **deliver** newspapers to every house on his street.

dentist (**den** tist) a doctor who takes care of your teeth
The **dentist** filled one cavity and then cleaned my teeth.

describe (de **scribe**) to draw a picture with words
Can you **describe** the boy who stole your bike?

desert (**des** ert) a large area of hot, dry, sandy land
The Sahara is a famous **desert** in Africa.

deserve (de **serve**) to have earned
Do you think you **deserve** a raise in your allowance?

desk a piece of furniture that you write and work at
He does his homework while seated at his **desk**.

dessert (des **sert**) a treat at the end of a meal
Last night at dinner we had chocolate pudding for **dessert**.

destroy (de **stroy**) to spoil completely, to wreck
A tornado can sometimes **destroy** a house.

detective (de **tec** tive) someone who tries to solve crimes
It took the **detective** two days to find the bank robber.

diagram (**di** a gram) a picture with labels that shows how something is made or works
The **diagram** helped us to put the model plane together.

dialogue (**di** alogue) a conversation between at least two people
In class Ann and I had a **dialogue** about the book we had read.

diamond (**di** a mond) 1. an expensive stone used in jewelry
An engagement ring usually has a **diamond** in it.
2. the infield area of a baseball field
He hit a home run and ran around all the bases on the **diamond**.
3. one of the four groups in a deck of playing cards
The heart and **diamond** cards are always red.

diary (**di** a ry) a written daily record
My sister keeps her **diary** locked up in her desk.

dictionary (**dic** tion ar y) a book that tells what words mean
The big **dictionary** in the library has every word in the English language.

diet (**di** et) to eat special foods, usually in order to lose weight
It was hard for Kathy to **diet** while her friends were always eating candy.

different (**dif** fer ent) not the same, unlike
Although they are twins, they are very **different** from each other.

difficult (**dif** fi cult) hard, complicated
Ice skating seemed so **difficult** at first, but now it is easy.

dig to scoop out and make a hole
A gardener has to **dig** up the earth before he can plant the seeds.

dinner (**din** ner) the main meal of the day
At our house, we always eat **dinner** when my father comes home from work.

dinosaur (**di** no saur) a kind of gigantic reptile that lived and died out millions of years ago
It's impossible to see a living **dinosaur** today, but you can see an exhibit of dinosaur bones at a museum.

direct (di **rect**) to guide, to lead
He had to **direct** all traffic away from the accident.

direction (di **rec** tion) 1. a way to go
Did you see which **direction**
my friend just took?
2. an instruction, a
command
We didn't open the test
booklet until the teacher gave
the **direction** to begin.

dirty (**dirt** y) not clean, soiled
We put all the **dirty** beach towels into the washing machine.

disagree (dis a **gree**) to have a different opinion
Billy and I don't get along because we **disagree** about
everything.

disappear (dis ap **pear**) to go out of sight
The magician put the lady in the box and made her
disappear.

discotheque (**dis** co theque) a club where people
dance to music
She knew her friends loved to dance, so she held her birthday
party at a **discotheque**.

discover (dis **cov** er) to find something for the first
time
The telescope helped Galileo **discover** the moons of Jupiter.

discuss (dis **cuss**) to talk over

Let's **discuss** your feelings about summer camp before you decide whether or not to go.

disease (dis **ease**) a sickness, an illness

Polio used to be a bad childhood **disease** until Dr. Jonas Salk discovered the vaccine that prevents it.

disguise (dis **guise**) something that changes your looks

The crook wore a **disguise** so that no one would be able to identify him.

dismiss (dis **miss**) to let go, to send away

The teacher said she would **dismiss** us right after the math test.

display (dis **play**) to show, to exhibit

We're proud to **display** our country's flag in front of the United Nations building.

distance (**dis** tance) the space between two points

It's a short **distance** from the school to the library.

distribute (dis **trib** ute) to hand out

Mike stopped to **distribute** the fliers to everyone at the bus stop.

disturb (dis **turb**) to upset

She hoped no one would **disturb** her while she studied.

dive to jump headfirst into water
The lifeguard never lets us **dive** into the shallow end of the pool.

divide (di **vide**) to separate into smaller parts
We asked him to **divide** the pizza into six equal slices.

divorce (di **vorce**) to end a marriage legally, to separate
Buddy told me that his parents were going to **divorce**.

dizzy (**diz** zy) unsteady from spinning
I feel **dizzy** just watching some of the rides at the amusement park.

doctor (**doc** tor) a person trained to treat our illnesses and injuries and to check our health
Every player had to be examined by the **doctor** before joining the team.

doll a kind of toy that usually looks like a person or animal
She spoke to her **doll** the way her mother spoke to the baby.

dope 1. a stupid person
It is nasty to call anyone a **dope**.
2. a dangerous drug
Say no to **dope**.

double (**dou** ble) twice as much

If Debbie would do more chores around the house, they would give her **double** her allowance.

doughnut (**dough** nut) a small round cake that is fried in oil

I like a **doughnut** that is filled with jelly, but my brother likes one with a hole in the middle.

dozen (**doz** en) twelve of something

If you buy a **dozen** doughnuts, you get a thirteenth free.

drag to pull along

It took two of us to **drag** the heavy trunk to the front door.

dragon (**drag** on) a make-believe monster that looks like a reptile with wings

In my book about Saint George, the pictures show a **dragon** breathing fire.

draw 1. to make a picture

Everyone stopped to watch the man **draw** with chalk on the sidewalk.

2. to pull, to drag

The farmer used a rope to **draw** a bucket of water from the well.

dream the pictures and stories that you imagine while sleeping

A scary **dream** is called a nightmare.

drink to swallow liquid

I'd rather **drink** orange juice than eat an orange.

drive to steer a moving car

When you are old enough, you can learn to **drive**.

drop to let fall

If you **drop** that tray, the water will spill all over everything.

drown to die underwater

Without air tanks, a deep-sea diver would **drown**.

dry 1. not wet

I changed to **dry** clothing after coming in out of the rain.

2. thirsty

We were so **dry** after hiking that we each drank a whole bottle of soda.

dull 1. boring, uninteresting

Tim gave such a **dull** book report that we all started falling asleep.

2. not sharp

It is hard to write with a **dull** pencil point.

dumb 1. not able to speak, mute

Deaf children are often **dumb**.

2. stupid

Spilling that bottle of expensive perfume was a **dumb** thing to do.

dump to unload, to throw away

There soon won't be any room to **dump** all the garbage we make every day.

dwarf a person who is much smaller than normal

A **dwarf** needs to buy special clothes.

Ee

eager (**ea** ger) wanting, enthusiastic
He was so **eager** to go fishing that he woke up at four o'clock in the morning.

ear the part of the body we hear with
The doctor fitted Grandma with a hearing aid for her left **ear**.

early (**ear** ly) before the expected time
We got to the ballpark **early** so we could practice before the game.

earn to work for, to deserve
He spent long hours at the factory to **earn** more money for his family.

1. Earth the planet we live on
Astronauts are the only people who have ever left **Earth**.

2. earth soil, ground
We dug holes in the **earth** to plant the baby trees.

earthquake (**earth** quake) a shaking of some section of the earth or ground
In a bad **earthquake,** the ground trembles and buildings fall.

easel (**ea** sel) a stand that holds or displays a picture
I left my painting on the **easel** to dry.

easy (**eas** y) simple, not difficult
It was **easy** to find our way from the train station to the hotel.

eat to swallow food
We snack when we **eat** between meals.

edge 1. the place where something ends
The Ping-Pong ball hit the **edge** of the table and bounced off.
2. the sharp side of a blade
He cut himself on the **edge** of the knife.

elect (e **lect**) to choose by voting
In our city, we **elect** a mayor every four years.

electricity (e lec **tric** i ty) a kind of energy that comes through wires and makes things work
People used candles for light before they discovered that **electricity** could make light bulbs glow.

elephant (**el** e phant) a kind of large land animal that has big ears and a long trunk
The **elephant** was trained to lie down when the little girl tapped its side.

elevator (**el** e va tor) a moving compartment that takes people up and down in a building
I took the **elevator** to the fourth floor.

embarrassed (em **bar** rassed) ashamed
I was **embarrassed** when I forgot my lines in the play.

emergency (e **mer** gen cy) an unexpected happening that needs immediate attention, a crisis
>We all should know telephone numbers to call in case of **emergency**.

empty (**emp** ty) having nothing inside
>We took the **empty** soda bottles back to the store.

encyclopedia (en cy clo **pe** di a) a set of books with information on many topics
>I looked in the "C" volume of my **encyclopedia** to find out more about Canada.

end the last part
>The **end** of that story was very sad.

enemy (**en** e my) a person or group on the opposite side of a fight
>During color war, the Red Team is the **enemy**.

enjoy (en **joy**) to get pleasure from, to like
>Did you **enjoy** your vacation at the beach?

enter (**en** ter) to go into
>You cannot **enter** the theater without a ticket.

entertainment (en ter **tain** ment) some kind of amusement
>That hotel offered musical **entertainment** for teenagers as well as for adults.

equal (**e** qual) the same as
Two cups of milk are **equal** to one pint.

erase (e **rase**) to rub out
Please **erase** yesterday's work from the blackboard.

errand (**er** rand) a task that requires one to go somewhere
My mother gave me the **errand** of buying milk at the grocery.

error (**er** ror) a mistake
There is a spelling **error** in that letter you wrote.

escalator (**es** ca la tor) a moving stairway that takes people up and down
I'd rather take the **escalator** upstairs than wait for the elevator to come.

escape (es **cape**) to get away
The prisoner tried to **escape** by digging a tunnel under the fence.

Eskimo (**Es** ki mo) a member of a group that lives in very cold northern areas
The **Eskimo** left the igloo early in the morning to hunt and fish for food.

evaporate (e **vap** o rate) to change from a liquid to a gas
On a very hot day, a puddle of water will **evaporate** quickly and disappear.

76

even (**e** ven) 1. flat and smooth
> After a bumpy ride, she was glad when the ground became **even**.

2. same or equal
> The score was **even** after four innings.

event (e **vent**) something that takes place, a happening
> Columbus's discovery of America is the most famous **event** of 1492.

evil (**e** vil) bad, wicked
> In fairy tales, the stepmother who tricks the children is always **evil**.

exaggerate (ex **ag** ger ate) to stretch the truth in telling a story
> You **exaggerate** when you say the fish you caught was as big as a whale.

examine (ex **am** ine) to study closely, to look at carefully
> The doctor wanted to **examine** my leg to make sure it had healed.

example (ex **am** ple) a sample, a model
> Edward's homework was put up on the board as an **example** of perfect handwriting.

excellent (**ex** cel lent) very, very good
> The burgers we ate were good, but the french fries were **excellent**.

exciting (ex **cit** ing) not boring, full of action

The last few minutes of the game were so **exciting** that the whole crowd stood and cheered.

excuse (ex **cuse**) the explanation for why something was done wrong

What's your **excuse** for coming so late?

exercise (ex er cise) activity done to build a stronger body

Eddie's favorite **exercise** is jogging.

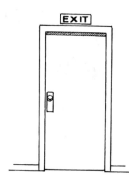

exhibit (ex **hib** it) a display, a showing

The post office has an interesting **exhibit** of Olympic stamps.

exit (**ex** it) a way out

An usher pointed the way to the side **exit** of the movie theater.

expect (ex **pect**) to think something will happen

I **expect** to get lots of birthday cards in the mail.

expensive (ex **pen** sive) costing a lot, high-priced

A new car was too **expensive,** so my father bought a used one.

experiment (ex **per** i ment) a test to find out something

We did an **experiment** to show which things a magnet will attract.

explain (ex **plain**) to tell what something means, to make clear

He had to **explain** that a battery works by creating an electrical circuit.

explore (ex **plore**) to look into something new, to investigate

On our hike, we stopped to **explore** a cave.

explosion (ex **plo** sion) a sudden burst with loud noise

That loud sound was caused by an **explosion** in the building.

extra (**ex** tra) more than needed, spare

The car had five tires — one on each of the four wheels and one **extra** in the trunk.

eye the part of the face we see with

A piece of dirt flew into my **eye** and made the tears start to flow.

Ff

factory (**fac** to ry) a place where things are made

We took a tour of the chocolate **factory** and saw how cocoa beans are turned into candy.

fail to be unsuccessful

If I don't practice some math problems, I'll **fail** that test tomorrow.

1. fair 1. honest and correct

A fight is **fair** only if it's one against one.

2. sunny, clear

He waited for the first **fair** day to take out the rowboat.

3. average

He got only a **fair** grade on his book report because of all the spelling errors.

2. fair a market and show set up for a short period of time

Grandma won first prize for her apple pie at the state **fair**.

fake not real, phony

The police knew he was not the robber when his gun turned out to be **fake**.

1. fall to drop, to come down

If you push it, the plate will **fall** off the edge of the table.

2. fall autumn

In the **fall,** the leaves change color and blow off the trees.

false 1. not true, incorrect

We had to mark every question on the geography test either true or **false.**

2. fake

Aunt Millie kept her **false** teeth in a glass at night.

family (**fam** i ly) a group of people related to each other

Your parents, brothers, sisters, grandparents, aunts, uncles, and cousins are all members of your **family.**

famous (**fa** mous) well-known

The Beatles were **famous,** for everyone in the world knew their rock-and-roll music.

fan 1. something that cools people or things by moving air

Our new electric **fan** makes a comfortable breeze on a hot day.

2. a person who is very interested in someone or something and follows it closely.

Jim is a big **fan** of baseball in the summer and hockey in the winter.

far not near, distant

Some stars are too **far** away to see without a telescope.

fare the money charged for riding from one place to another

Children only had to pay half the **fare** to ride the bus.

farm land that is used to raise crops and animals for food

Sometimes a **farm** is used to grow only corn.

fast quick

She was so **fast** that she finished the race far ahead of the others.

fat heavy, chubby

Jack Sprat was thin, but his wife was **fat**.

father (**fa** ther) a man who has a child

He's the **father** of two girls and two boys.

fault a mistake

Coloring the sky green was the only **fault** in my picture.

favor (**fa** vor) a good deed, a kindness

She did me a **favor** when she brought my book back to the library.

favorite (**fa** vor ite) best-liked

I can watch reruns of my **favorite** TV shows over and over again.

February (**Feb** ru ar y) the second month of the year

I'll bring you flowers and candy if you will be mine,
on that day in **February** called "St. Valentine."

feed to give food to

Will you **feed** my cat his dinner while I'm away?

female (**fe** male) a girl or a woman

My mother is a **female,** and so is my sister.

fence a kind of wall that keeps things apart, a gate

They built a **fence** around the yard to keep their neighbors outside and their dogs inside.

ferry (**fer** ry) a boat that carries people and cars across a small body of water

You have to take a **ferry** to get over the river from Manhattan to the Statue of Liberty.

fever (**fe** ver) a high body temperature

It's common for a sick person to have a **fever**.

few a small number

I'll meet you outside in a **few** minutes.

field a large open piece of land

The **field** was covered with grass and wildflowers.

fight 1. an argument

The **fight** got so loud that people turned around to listen.

2. a struggle

The two drivers had a **fight** over who should get the parking space in the mall.

fill to put in as much as a container will hold, to load
Fill the dish with candy before our company comes.

film 1. a special material put in a camera to take pictures
She used up a whole roll of **film** on our class trip.
2. a motion picture
They're shooting a **film** right here in town.

filthy (**filth** y) very, very dirty
My shoes got **filthy** from walking in the mud.

find to come upon, to discover
Everyone was trying to **find** unusual shells down by the shore.

fine 1. good, excellent
"Mona Lisa" is a **fine** work of art.
2. very thin, delicate
The baby's hair was too **fine** to put a bow in it.

finish (**fin** ish) to end
You **finish** a game of chess when you capture the other player's king.

fire the flames that appear when something burns
At first the fire fighters saw only smoke, but soon they saw **fire**.

firecracker (**fire** crack er) a small explosive that is used to make noise during celebrations
The sound of a **firecracker** on the Fourth of July made the puppy hide under the bed.

fireworks (**fire** works) firecrackers and other explosives that make noise and light up the sky

On Independence Day, **fireworks** fill the sky with red, white, and blue.

first before any others

George Washington was the **first** President of the United States.

fish a kind of animal that lives in water

We have skin and breathe through our mouths, but **fish** have scales and breathe through their gills.

fist a tightly closed hand

He held up his **fist** as a warning not to come any closer.

fit to be the right size for

I grew this summer, so my old coat will probably not **fit** me next winter.

fix to repair, to mend

The repairman will need his tools to **fix** the broken washing machine.

flag a banner with colors and symbols of a country or organization

The American **flag** has fifty stars and thirteen stripes.

flashlight (**flash** light) a small light powered by batteries, that can be carried around

Dad keeps a **flashlight** in the car in case he gets stuck at night.

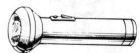

flat level, smooth

We rode up and down hills until we finally came to an area that was **flat**.

flavor (**fla** vor) the taste of something

Chocolate is my favorite **flavor** of ice cream.

float 1. to stay on top of water

The baby's rubber toys **float** in the bathtub.

2. to drift through the air

If you let go of that string, the balloon will **float** away.

flood an overflow of water

When the pipe burst, there was a **flood** in our basement.

floor 1. the bottom of a room

He tried to walk across the **floor,** but it had just been waxed and was too slippery.

2. a level or story of a building

His office is on the second **floor**.

flour a powder made from grain, that is used to make bread and cake

Mother sometimes sifts the **flour** to get the lumps out.

flower (**flow** er) the colorful part of a plant, the blossom

Each man in the wedding party wore a **flower** in his lapel.

fly 1. to move through the air on wings

The mother robin taught the baby birds to **fly** from the nest.

2. to ride in an airplane

The fastest way to travel from the East Coast to the West Coast is to **fly**.

fog a cloud or a mist near the ground

The **fog** was so thick that we could not see the road in front of us.

fold to bend paper or material

You must **fold** your clothes before you can put them in your suitcase.

folder (**fold** er) a sheet of cardboard, bent in half, that holds loose papers

My mother looked through my work **folder** on Open School Day.

follow (**fol** low) to come after

Because he couldn't keep up, Toto had to **follow** Dorothy down the yellow brick road.

food the things we eat

Hamburgers and salad were all the **food** we had for dinner.

foolish (**fool** ish) silly

Clowns appear to be **foolish** when they act in the circus, but they must study and work hard to be able to make people laugh.

football (**foot** ball) a sport played with an oval ball by two teams of eleven members each on a field with a goalpost at each end

The object of **football** is to carry the ball over the goal line to score a touchdown or to kick it through the goalposts for field goals and extra points.

foreigner (**for** eign er) someone from another country

I knew he was a **foreigner** by the way he spoke.

forest (**for** est) a large area with many trees, woods

They walked deep into the **forest,** picking berries from the trees.

forget (for **get**) to fail to remember

Though his mother reminded him, Harry did **forget** to buy a Father's Day card after all.

forgive (for **give**) to excuse, to pardon

I **forgive** you this time, but don't keep me waiting so long again.

fracture (**frac** ture) a break, a crack

They didn't know he had a **fracture** in his arm until it showed up on the X ray.

frame an open case for something, a border, an edge

We ordered a **frame** for our new picture.

free 1. costing nothing

> They gave away **free** caps at the baseball game.

2. not controlled by others

> How grand to live in a country where we are **free**!

freeze to turn hard from cold, to turn into ice

We have to wait for the lake to **freeze** before we can go ice skating.

fresh 1. just made

> The **fresh** bread was still hot from the oven.

2. new and clean

> They opened the windows to let some **fresh** air into the waiting room.

3. rude, impolite

> When he refused to answer the question, he was sent to the principal's office for being **fresh**.

friend someone you like and feel close to

My best **friend** and I play every day.

frighten (**fright** en) to scare

A big dog barking can really **frighten** you.

front the side facing forward

The **front** of the house usually has the biggest door and the most windows.

frozen (**fro** zen) as cold and hard as ice

We put the **frozen** TV dinners into the microwave and heated them.

fruit the part of a plant that we can eat

We visited an orchard where the farmer let us pick the **fruit** from the apple trees.

fry to cook in hot oil

In Boy Scout camp, we learned how to catch a fish, clean it, and **fry** it over a fire.

fun enjoyment, a good time

The best **fun** is a party where we play lots of games.

funny (**fun** ny) comical, amusing

That picture of the dog wearing a hat was **funny**.

fur the thick, soft hair of some animals

Bears need their **fur** to keep warm and dry.

future (**fu** ture) the time ahead of us

Some people think fortune-tellers can say what will happen in the **future**.

Gg

gamble (gam ble) to play a game for money

We decided to **gamble** on our card game, and I lost fifty cents.

game a fun activity with set rules that is played to win

When it started to rain, we switched from a **game** of baseball to a **game** of Monopoly.

gang a group of people who spend a lot of time together doing things that get them into trouble

The police came when they heard that the **gang** was writing graffiti in the schoolyard.

gangster (gang ster) a person who belongs to a gang, a criminal

The police proved that he was a **gangster** who committed many crimes with his partners.

garage (gar **age**) a building where cars are kept

The **garage** next to our house is big enough for two cars.

garbage (gar bage) things that are thrown away, trash

We keep our **garbage** in big cans until the sanitation workers pick it up.

garden (**gar** den) a piece of land where flowers or vegetables are grown

The tomatoes from our **garden** taste much better than the ones from the supermarket.

gasoline (gas o **line**) the liquid fuel that makes cars and planes go

Many people have learned to pump their own **gasoline** at self-service gas stations.

gate a swinging door that lets people in or out

There's always a guard at the zoo **gate** to make sure you have bought your ticket.

generous (**gen** er ous) happy to give or to share with others, unselfish

Mom is always **generous** in handing out treats when I have friends sleep over.

genius (**gen** ius) a person with a great mind

Thomas Edison was a **genius** who invented light bulbs and recorded sound.

gentle (**gen** tle) mild, kind

She was very **gentle** as she carefully held and fed the newborn puppy.

geography (ge **og** ra phy) the study of life over all the different parts of Earth

In studying **geography,** we often discuss the various climates of the world.

ghost the imaginary spirit of a dead person

I dressed up like a **ghost** last Halloween, even though I know there's no such thing.

giant (**gi** ant) an imaginary very large person

At the top of the beanstalk, Jack met a cruel **giant** ten times as big as he.

gift a present

The **gift** was wrapped in fancy paper and a big red ribbon.

gigantic (gi **gan** tic) very large, huge

We saw **gigantic** redwood trees on our trip to California.

giggle (**gig** gle) to laugh in a silly way

Did you hear the baby **giggle** when I tickled him?

glad happy, pleased

I was **glad** to hear you would be coming to the party.

glass 1. a hard material that you can see through

When the window broke, the **glass** from it shattered all over the floor

2. a drinking container made of that hard breakable material

Would you like me to pour some ice-cold lemonade into a **glass** for you?

globe a round map of Earth

A **globe** is really a small model of our entire world.

glove a kind of clothing that covers the hand, with a space for each finger

I had a **glove** to keep my right hand warm, but I'd lost the one for my left hand.

glue a sticky liquid that is used to hold things together

The strong **glue** held the new mirror on his bike.

goal something you want and try to reach, an aim

Their **goal** was to collect one hundred dollars for the library.

gold a yellow metal that is used to make expensive jewelry

They bought Peter a watch made of **gold** for his graduation.

grab to snatch

If you **grab** the ball from the dog's mouth, the dog will growl at you.

graceful (**grace** ful) beautiful and easy in movement

All the ballet dancers were so **graceful**.

grade 1. a mark, a score

His **grade** on the arithmetic test was a "B."

2. a school level

He was held back and had to repeat the third **grade**.

graduate (**grad** u ate) to complete a school's program and receive a diploma

After I **graduate** from elementary school, I'll go on to junior high school.

grandfather (**grand** fa ther) the father of one's father or mother

My **grandfather** is twenty-five years older than my father.

grandmother (**grand** moth er) the mother of one's father or mother

I visit one **grandmother** every summer vacation, but my other **grandmother** lives with us.

great   1. very good, wonderful

We had a **great** vacation when we visited beautiful Niagara Falls for the first time.

2. very important

The faces of some of our **great** presidents are printed on our bills and coins.

grocery (**gro** cer y) a store that sells foods and other household supplies

The little **grocery** closed down when the big supermarket opened across the street.

grouch someone who is cranky or cross

After his team lost, he acted like a **grouch** by frowning and grumbling for the rest of the day.

ground the surface of Earth, the soil

She dug many holes in the **ground** and planted tulip bulbs in them.

group a number of people or things that are together

There must be fifty tourists in the **group** that just got off that plane.

grow to get bigger

The gardener said that little tree would **grow** to be six feet tall.

grown-up an adult

Anyone under thirteen needs a **grown-up** to take them into that movie.

guarantee (guar an **tee**) to promise, to assure

The salesman said the company would **guarantee** that the TV set would work for five years.

guard to protect, to watch over

The museum needs many people to **guard** its paintings from thieves.

guess to try to answer some question without knowing the answer

He can **guess** your weight without lifting you.

guest a visitor in someone's home or in a hotel

The management sent a basket of fruit to each **guest** who came to stay.

guide someone who shows the way, a leader
The **guide** of our tour led us through the noisy bazaar.

guilty (**guilt** y) at fault
The judge said he was **guilty** of the crime and sentenced him to a year in jail.

gun a weapon that shoots
The loud bang of his **gun** marked the start of the race.

gym a place where people exercise and play sports
A fighter runs and lifts weights in the **gym** every day before he goes into the ring.

Hh

habit (**hab** it) something done so often that it becomes a regular pattern

Terry had a **habit** of biting his nails whenever he felt nervous.

half one of two equal parts

We cut the sandwich down the middle and each ate a **half**.

hall a passageway in a building, a corridor

Walking through the **hall** is the only way to get from one classroom to another.

Halloween (Hal low **een**) the night of October 31, when people dress up in costumes

On **Halloween,** we all trick-or-treat and collect candy from the neighbors.

hammer (**ham** mer) a tool used to drive nails

We use a **hammer** to nail picture hooks to the wall.

handkerchief (**hand** ker chief) a small square of cloth used to wipe the nose

Some people use tissues, but I prefer a **handkerchief**.

handle (**han** dle) the part made for holding something

The saleslady put a **handle** on the box so that we could carry it easily.

handsome (**hand** some) good-looking

She was a beautiful bride, and he was a **handsome** groom.

handy (**hand** y) 1. ready, useful

When I went to the rock concert, I kept a pen **handy** for the group's autographs.

2. able to fix things easily, skilled

My father is **handy,** so he never has to call a repairman for his car.

happen (**hap** pen) to take place

The shuttle launch was carefully planned so it would **happen** on time.

happy (**hap** py) glad, joyful

My dog wags his tail and licks my face because he is **happy** to see me come home from summer camp.

hard 1. firm, solid

Cement is wet and soft when it's poured, but when it dries it turns **hard**.

2. difficult, tough

The test was so **hard** that a few of my friends failed it.

harm to hurt

You can **harm** zoo animals by feeding them the wrong foods.

harvest (**har** vest) to gather a crop

The farmers **harvest** ripe pumpkins in the fall.

hatch to break out of an egg

When they start to **hatch,** baby chicks peck through their shells with their hard little beaks.

hate to dislike very much

I love having a dog, but I **hate** walking him early in the morning.

haunted (**haunt** ed) taken over by ghosts, spooky

The strange flickering lights and eerie laughter made us think the house was **haunted**.

headline (**head** line) the words in large print at the top of a newspaper or an article

The sports **headline** in today's newspaper announced the winner of the boxing match and new heavyweight champion of the world.

heal to cure

A clean bandage can help **heal** the cut on your hand.

healthy (**health** y) in good condition, not sick

You must be strong and **healthy** to get on a school football team.

heart 1. an organ of the body, in the chest, that pumps blood

When he ran, he could feel his **heart** pounding quickly.

2. a shape that stands for love

I cut out a big red **heart** and pasted it on a Valentine's Day card.

heavy (**heav** y) weighing a lot
It took three men to lift that **heavy** piano into our new house.

height how high or how tall something or someone is
Dave grew four inches in **height** in just one year.

helicopter (**hel** i cop ter) a type of aircraft with no wings and a propellor on top
In a large city, a **helicopter** is used to fly over busy roads and report on traffic conditions.

helmet (**hel** met) a hard hat worn by ballplayers, construction workers, soldiers, and others
Every welder wears a **helmet** to protect him from falling building material.

help to assist, to be useful
Could you **help** me lift this heavy ladder?

herd a group of animals that stay together
The cowboy led the **herd** of cattle out to pasture.

hermit (**her** mit) someone who chooses to live away from other people
He became a **hermit** and stayed all alone in the woods.

hero (**he** ro) someone we respect for his bravery
The lifeguard became a **hero** when he saved the girl from drowning.

hide to put out of sight

We don't want a stranger to find our extra house key, so we always **hide** it under the mat near the door.

highway (**high** way) a main road

The **highway** passes through all the major cities in our state.

hike a long walk that often includes some climbing

The Boy Scouts planned a **hike** up the mountain before their cookout.

hill a raised area of land

It's fun to ride my bike down a steep **hill,** but I have to walk it back up.

hint a clue

"Is it bigger than a bread box?" I said, asking for a **hint**.

hire 1. to give a job to, to employ

The manager promised to **hire** my brother to work after school.

2. to rent or lease

They had to **hire** a hall for the high school prom.

history (**his** to ry) the story of things that happened in the past

The **history** of our country starts with the discovery of America by Columbus.

hit to strike

The champ **hit** him so hard that he was knocked out in the first round.

hitchhike (**hitch** hike) to get a free ride with a stranger

Though he'd been warned it was something a person should never do, he tried to **hitchhike** back into town.

hobby (**hob** by) an activity someone likes to do in his spare time

Alan's **hobby** is collecting stamps.

hold 1. to keep or carry in your hand

Hold my books while I tie my sneaker.

2. to have room for

Our school bus can **hold** thirty-three kids.

holdup (**hold** up) a robbery

There was another **holdup** in the bank by two men with guns.

hole an empty space, an opening

After he stepped on a nail, there was a **hole** in his shoe.

holiday (**hol** i day) a special day of rest or celebration

On a **holiday** like New Year's Day, most people have time off from work and from school.

home the place where one lives

A bear makes his winter **home** in a cave.

homesick (**home** sick) feeling sad and lonely when away from home

I wasn't **homesick** at camp until my parents came up on visiting day.

homework (**home** work) the schoolwork you do at home
> It takes me about half an hour to do my arithmetic **homework** every night.

honest (**hon** est) truthful, law-abiding
> All the money was still in her wallet, so she knew the man who had returned it was **honest**.

honey (**hon** ey) a thick, sweet liquid made by bees
> My grandmother likes **honey** on her pancakes for breakfast.

hop to do a short jump, sometimes on one foot
> In one of the relay races in gym, we have to **hop** across the floor.

hope to wish that something would happen
> I **hope** that my pen pal may come to visit me someday.

horn 1. a hard, pointed part of the heads of some animals
>> A bull's **horn** is much longer than a goat's.
> 2. a car's warning signal that makes a loud noise
>> The driver sounded the **horn** when the child ran into the street.
> 3. a kind of musical instrument
>> The tuba is my favorite type of **horn** in the parade.

horrible (**hor** ri ble) terrible, awful
> I woke up crying from a **horrible** dream last night.

horse a kind of large animal used for riding, pulling heavy loads, and races

The groom brushed the mane and tail of the **horse** before every race.

hose a soft tube used to carry liquids or air

The fire fighters put out the flames by pumping water through the **hose**.

hospital (**hos** pi tal) a building where sick and injured people are taken care of

We visited Bill in the **hospital,** where he'd had his tonsils removed.

hostage (**hos** tage) someone held prisoner by people who won't let him go until they get what they want

The bank robber took a teller as **hostage** until he could get away safely.

hot 1. very warm, having a high temperature

The weather was so **hot** that we had to use the air conditioner both in the house and in the car.

2. spicy

Though its temperature is cold, gazpacho's flavor is **hot**.

hotel (ho **tel**) a building with rooms that people pay to stay in when away from home

When we realized that we would not arrive at Grandma's till tomorrow, we checked into a **hotel** for the night.

hour sixty minutes

From noon to one o'clock in the afternoon is one **hour**.

house a building where people live

Mom and Dad just bought a two-story **house** with three bedrooms upstairs.

hug to put the arms around

The baby likes to **hug** me when I pick her up.

huge very big, gigantic

We flew home on a **huge** plane that held four hundred people.

humorous (**hu** mor ous) funny, comical

He's fun at parties because he tells such **humorous** stories.

hungry (**hun** gry) wanting food

I was so **hungry** that I ate two sandwiches with my soda.

hunt to look for, to search for

Cavemen had to **hunt** animals they could kill for food and clothing.

hurricane (**hur** ri cane) a very big storm with winds and rain

Everyone in town boarded up the windows when they heard the **hurricane** was coming.

hurry (**hur** ry) to move quickly, to rush

If I **hurry**, I'll catch the next train.

hurt to injure, to harm

I **hurt** my knee when I fell on the ice.

husband (**hus** band) a man who is married

After their wedding, he was no longer her boyfriend but her **husband**.

hut a simply made house, a shack

We saw a film about a poor family that lived in a **hut**.

hydrant (**hy** drant) an outside connection to underground water pipes

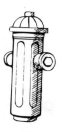

The fire fighters connected the hose to the **hydrant** right outside the burning building.

hypnotize (**hyp** no tize) to put someone under a spell so that he will follow your directions

He had to **hypnotize** my mother so that he could order her to stop smoking.

Ii

ice water that is frozen

The melting snow turned to **ice** when the temperature dropped.

ice cream a sweet frozen dessert

I like to eat **ice cream** in a cone.

icing (**ic** ing) the frosting on a cake

When my mother makes a cake, she lets me lick the **icing** off the mixing spoon.

idea (i **de** a) an original thought

It was my **idea** to trade comic books every few weeks.

identical (i **den** ti cal) exactly the same

The twins were **identical,** and I couldn't tell them apart.

igloo (**ig** loo) an Eskimo house made of ice and snow

The top of an **igloo** is usually round like a dome.

ignore (ig **nore**) to pay no attention to, to avoid

If we **ignore** that bully, he'll stop teasing us.

ill sick

He felt **ill** after eating too much candy.

illustration (il lus **tra** tion) a picture that makes something easier to understand

My scooter came with an **illustration** that shows how to put the parts together.

imagine (i **mag** ine) to think about something and picture it, to daydream

When I **imagine** what it would be like to live at the North Pole, I see snow and ice everywhere.

imitate (**im** i tate) to copy someone

To **imitate** the man taking a picture, the monkey put its hand in front of its face and looked at us for a long time.

immediately (im **me** di ate ly) right away, at once

When she found out I hadn't done my homework, my mother called to tell me to come home **immediately**.

impatient (im **pa** tient) unable to wait calmly, restless

We got so **impatient** waiting for the bus that we decided to walk to the library.

impolite (im po **lite**) rude, ill-mannered

The old woman on the bus told Bobby it was **impolite** for him to sit while she stood.

important (im **por** tant) mattering a great deal, meaningful

Our President holds the most **important** office in our country.

impossible (im **pos** si ble) not able to happen
It's **impossible** for all ten of us to get into one little car.

improve (im **prove**) to make or get better
She needed a tutor to help her **improve** in math.

include (in **clude**) to make part of
Did you **include** the basket in the price of this bike?

increase (in **crease**) to make bigger, to enlarge
George is lifting weights to **increase** the size of his chest and his upper arms.

indoors (in **doors**) inside a building
It rained, so we had to stay **indoors**.

infant (**in** fant) a baby
Because the **infant** could not yet walk, the woman had to carry him.

inflate (in **f late**) to blow up with air
I used the air pump at the gas station to **inflate** the tires of my bike.

information (in for **ma** tion) the facts about some matter
I used an encyclopedia to get **information** about Native Americans.

ingredient (in **gre** di ent) one item in a mixture
Tuna is the most important **ingredient** in tuna casserole.

injection (in **jec** tion) a dose of medicine given with a needle

After the dog bit me, I needed an **injection** every day for a week.

injure (**in** jure) to hurt, to damage

He could **injure** his pitching arm if he keeps throwing so hard.

innocent (**in** no cent) not guilty

By showing that he was far away on the day of the crime, he proved that he was **innocent**.

insane (in **sane**) mentally ill, crazy

There's a special hospital in our town just to treat the **insane**.

inspect (in **spect**) to examine carefully

Before he bought the car, my father wanted someone to **inspect** it to make sure it was safe.

instrument (**in** stru ment) 1. a tool that is used to do some work

A nurse hands my dentist the **instrument** he needs to clean my teeth.

2. something that makes music

The tambourine was the only **instrument** I ever learned to play in school.

intelligent (in **tel** li gent) smart, bright
The kids in that family are so **intelligent** that they're all in advanced classes.

interesting (**in** ter est ing) holding one's attention
I read book after book about dinosaurs, because I find them to be the most **interesting** animals ever.

interfere (in ter **fere**) to come in between, to meddle
I had to **interfere** when they couldn't settle the argument themselves.

intermission (in ter **mis** sion) a break, a recess
There were two acts in the play, and we had an **intermission** between them.

interrupt (in ter **rupt**) to break in, to interfere
Interrupt me with questions if I say something you don't understand.

interview (**in** ter view) to question for information
I asked the principal if I could **interview** her for the school newspaper.

introduce (in tro **duce**) to present for the first time
I wanted to **introduce** my two best friends so they could get to know each other.

invent (in **vent**) to make up something for the first time, to create
Alexander Graham Bell did **invent** the telephone.

investigate (in **ves** ti gate) to look into something to get the facts

My parents want to **investigate** that organization before they donate money.

invisible (in **vis** i ble) not able to be seen

If I were **invisible,** no one would know I'd dropped that easy fly ball.

invite (in **vite**) to ask someone to come somewhere

How many people do you plan to **invite** to your party?

iron (**i** ron) 1. a hard, strong metal

      Iron is used to make the steel in the beams that hold up buildings.

    2. a tool that is used when hot, to take creases out of clothing

      Jenny wanted to use the **iron** on her dress, but my mother was afraid she'd burn herself.

island (**is** land) a piece of land with water on all sides

The man swam to a small **island** when his boat started to sink.

itch a feeling on the skin that makes you want to scratch

I couldn't reach the **itch** on my back.

Jj

jail a building where criminals are kept locked up
In a workroom in the **jail,** prisoners make the license plates for cars.

jam fruit and sugar cooked into a thick spread
When berries are in season, my mother makes her own **jam** and puts it in jars.

janitor (**jan** i tor) a worker who cleans and takes care of a building
The **janitor** was mopping the halls before classes started.

January (**Jan** u ar y) the first month of the year
January is here, it's snowy and freezing;
all of us kids are coughing and sneezing.

jar a small glass container that has a wide opening
The apricot jam came in a **jar**.

jaywalk (**jay** walk) to cross in the middle of a street or without a green light
If you **jaywalk,** you may get hit by a car.

jealous (**jeal** ous) wishing you had what someone else has, envious
Henry was **jealous** of my new bike until he got his own bike for Christmas.

114

jeans denim pants

We were not allowed to wear **jeans** to graduation.

jelly (**jel** ly) fruit juices and sugar cooked together

Jelly tastes great on a sandwich with peanut butter.

jet a fast plane that has no propellors

Nowadays only a jumbo **jet** carries passengers across the ocean; a smaller **jet** may be used as a fighter plane.

job 1. regular work, employment

Wally got a **job** delivering newspapers before school.

2. some task that has to be done, a chore

Ted's **job** was to clean the erasers.

jog to run slowly for exercise

The coach makes us all **jog** around the track three times before every game.

join 1. to bring together, to connect

In square dancing, we all **join** hands to form a circle.

2. to become a member of, to belong to

I learned to play the flute so I could **join** the school band this year.

joke a funny story

We had heard Grandpa's **joke** before, but we laughed anyway.

journey (**jour** ney) a long trip

The early settlers made the **journey** to the West in covered wagons.

joy happiness, delight

She jumped for **joy** when she won the spelling bee.

judge a person who makes a decision in a contest or in a court of law

The **judge** has a gavel, or a small hammer, so he can pound on his desk and get the attention of the people in the courtroom.

juggle (**jug** gle) to continue to throw a few things up in the air without dropping any

He could **juggle** three Indian clubs at the same time.

July (Ju **ly**) the seventh month of the year

The flags fly high on the Fourth of **July**.

jump to leap into the air

It was fun to **jump** up and down on the trampoline.

June the sixth month of the year

In **June,** school is over until the next fall;
that gives us some time to swim and play ball.

jungle (**jun** gle) a tropical place with lots of trees, plants, and wild animals

The thick growth of leaves and vines keeps the **jungle** dark at all times.

junk old useless stuff, trash

Broken toys and puzzles with missing pieces were some of the **junk** in our attic.

jury (**jur** y) a group of people who decide a case in a courtroom

A **jury** is usually made up of twelve people.

Kk

kangaroo (kan ga **roo**) a kind of Australian animal that leaps on its strong back legs

The **kangaroo** mother carries the baby in a pocket or pouch outside of her stomach.

karate (ka **ra** te) a way of fighting or defense that uses the hands and feet as the only weapons

Karate is a martial art that comes to us from the Far East.

keep 1. to store

I usually **keep** an extra pair of gym socks in my locker.

2. to own, to have for a time

When I saw the picture he took of me, I wanted to **keep** it forever.

key 1. a piece of metal cut out to fit some lock

I carry a **key** to my door, a **key** to my bike chain, and a **key** to my locker.

2. a clue, an explanation

The butler's broken watch was the **key** to the mystery.

3. a part of a piano that plays a note

The music teacher touched a **key** on the piano to start our song.

kick to strike with the foot

One player was able to **kick** the football right through the goalposts.

1. kid a child, a young person

When he saw I was a **kid,** he let me pay half fare to ride the bus.

2. kid to tease, to fool

He tried to **kid** me by disguising his voice on the telephone.

kidnap (**kid** nap) to take someone away and not let him return home

They wanted to **kidnap** the baby so they could ask the parents for thousands of dollars to bring her back.

kill to cause the death of, to destroy

Another bad fire could **kill** the rest of the trees in the forest.

kind helpful, thoughtful

It was **kind** of her to drive the old man to his doctor's appointment.

king the male ruler of a country

In England, the son of a **king** or queen becomes the next **king.**

kitchen (**kitch** en) the room where food is stored, prepared, and eaten

The refrigerator, the stove, and all the pots and pans are in the **kitchen**.

kite a light toy that sails through the air on a string

A windy day in March is the best time to fly a **kite**.

kneel to bend down on your knees

A camel is so tall that it must **kneel** before you can mount it for a ride.

knife a tool for cutting that has a sharp edge and a handle

He carved his initials in that tree with a **knife**.

knob a rounded handle

There was a **knob** on the kitchen drawer so we could pull it open.

knock to hit with the fist

The doorbell is broken, so **knock** on the door when you want to come in.

knot a tight twist of rope or string

The sailor uses a special **knot** for tying the ship up to the dock.

know to be familiar with

Do you **know** your multiplication tables?

Ll

label (**la** bel) a tag with information
I found the **label** that told the price of the shirt.

ladder (**lad** der) a set of steps that can be moved
from place to place
The librarian needed the **ladder** to reach the books on the top
shelf.

lake a still body of water surrounded by land
We can row, fish, *and* swim in a **lake**.

land 1. the solid part of Earth not covered by
water
We had been so many days out on the ocean that we
were thrilled to see dry **land**.
2. a country
My grandfather left his native **land** to come to
America.

landlord (**land** lord) a man who rents his property to
other people
We send our rent to the **landlord** on the first day of every
month.

language (**lan** guage) the words used by people,
often different in different countries of the world
When Juan first came from Puerto Rico, the only **language** he
knew was Spanish.

large big in amount or size

The piano was so **large** that the moving men couldn't fit it through the door.

lasso (**las** so) a rope with a loop at one end

The cowgirl twirled her **lasso** and threw it over the neck of the wild horse.

last after all others

Once all the customers had left, he was the **last** person in the bank.

late after the expected time

He got there **late,** so he missed the beginning of the film.

laugh to make a happy sound while smiling

I like to **laugh** when I hear something funny.

laundry (**laun** dry) 1. a place where clothing is washed and dried

We use the **laundry** in town because we don't have our own washer and dryer.

2. clothing that needs to be washed or has just been washed

I put the **laundry** in the washing machine, and my sister puts it in the dryer and folds it.

law a rule made by a government for all their people to follow

No one seems to know that there's a **law** against jaywalking.

lazy (**la** zy) unwilling to work

He failed the test because he was too **lazy** to study.

lead 1. to show the way, to guide

He used a flashlight to **lead** the way through the dark tunnel.

2. to be winning, to be ahead of the others

Which teams **lead** in the play-offs this year?

lean to rest against something or someone

If you **lean** against the rail that was just painted, you will get paint on your clothes.

learn to find out, to come to know

Did it take you long to **learn** how to use your computer?

leash a strap or chain for a pet

Pull on your dog's **leash** if you want him to stop.

least fewest, smallest in number

I have to admit that I chose to read the book with the **least** pages.

leave 1. to go away, to depart

She had to **leave** home early in order to arrive at her baby-sitting job on time.

2. to let stay

We'll by eating soon, so don't **leave** your books on the table.

lecture (**lec** ture) a speech that teaches

We all got a **lecture** on carelessness when my mother found the door unlocked in the morning.

leisure (**lei** sure) the free time to do whatever you like

I don't have much **leisure** between school, homework, and music lessons.

lend to let someone borrow something that must be returned

I will **lend** you my typewriter until next Friday.

length how long something is

A mile is 5,280 feet in **length.**

less not as much as

I make **less** money than she does, because she works more hours.

lesson (**les** son) something to be learned, an exercise

The right way to fall was the first **lesson** in skiing.

let to allow, to permit

Though Robbie had homework, his father **let** him go bowling with us last night.

letter (**let** ter) 1. one member of the alphabet

The name Mary starts with the **letter** M.

2. a message written on a piece of paper

I sent you a **letter** about my trip to France.

liar (**li** ar) a person who tells stories that are not true

Pinocchio's nose grew long because he was a **liar.**

liberty (**lib** er ty) freedom

The Declaration of Independence says that **liberty** is a natural right of all people.

library (**li** brar y) a place where a large collection of books is kept

I visit the **library** every week and borrow at least two books each time.

license (**li** cense) the written permission to do something

The police officer pulled him over for speeding and asked if he had a **license** to drive.

lid a cover, a top

Screw the **lid** tightly on the jar so that nothing spills out.

lifeguard (**life** guard) someone who looks after the safety of swimmers

The **lifeguard** watches people in the ocean and swims out to rescue anyone who needs help.

lift to pick up, to raise

Two men had to **lift** the sofa while the other laid the carpet under it.

light 1. not dark, bright

It is **light** enough in here to take a picture without a flashbulb.

2. not heavy

The grocery bags were **light** enough for me to carry home alone.

lightning (**light** ning) an electrical flash in the sky, caused by weather

Lightning can be frightening — and dangerous, too!

like 1. to enjoy

We all **like** cowboy movies best.

2. to be fond of

A friend is someone you **like**.

line 1. a long mark made with a writing tool

Make two columns on your paper by drawing a straight **line** down the center.

2. a row of people or things

We had to wait in **line** to get on the roller coaster.

3. a special kind of rope or wire

The telephone **line** is held up by wooden posts along the road.

4. a bus or subway route

The bus driver told us we had to change to another **line** to get to the stadium.

lion (**li** on) a large animal known as the king of the cat family

You could tell it was a male **lion** by its thick, shaggy mane.

liquid (**liq** uid) something that flows, that is not a gas or a solid

The only **liquid** I give my dog is water.

list a column of things that go together

I made a **list** of the clothing that I needed for camp.

listen (**lis** ten) to use your ears to hear something

Did you **listen** to the President's speech last night?

little (**lit** tle) small

An elephant is big, and a mouse is **little**.

lively (**live** ly) active, energetic

Everyone stopped to watch the **lively** puppy jumping and barking in the pet shop window.

load to fill, to pack

You must **load** your camera with film before you can take pictures.

lobby (**lob** by) the front waiting area in a building

A bellhop carried our luggage into the **lobby** of the hotel.

location (lo **ca** tion) the place where something is

The **location** of the store is the corner of Main Street and Oak Avenue.

lock to fasten, to shut tight

The last person out should **lock** the door so no one can get in.

locker (**lock** er) a small metal closet used to store things for a short time

I keep my school clothes in a **locker** during gym class.

lonely (**lone** ly) alone and sad

My little brother was **lonely** when we all left for school and he had to stay home.

look 1. to use your eyes to see something

I like to have the window seat on a plane so that I can **look** out at the world below.

2. to seem, to appear

Does it **look** as if we'll have enough kids for a game tomorrow?

loose not tight

Her scarf flew away because the knot was too **loose**.

lose 1. to misplace, to be unable to find

I always seem to **lose** one glove.

2. to fail to win

If we **lose** the race today, the other team will be the champs.

loud noisy

Our neighbor complained about the **loud** music coming from my stereo.

love to feel affection for, to adore

I like to help care for and play with my baby sister because I **love** her.

loyal (**loy** al) faithful to someone or something
A **loyal** friend will help him to get out of trouble.

lucky (**luck** y) fortunate
Pamela was **lucky** to win that big teddy bear at the fair.

lunch the midday meal
On the weekend, we always eat **lunch** at noon.

Mm

machine (ma **chine**) something that is built to do a job

A typewriter is a **machine** that writes.

mad 1. insane, crazy

He began to throw things around the room as if he were **mad**.

2. angry

I was really **mad** at Jack for not returning my typewriter last Friday.

magazine (mag a **zine**) a collection of stories and pictures that is published regularly

Each week there are new articles in my favorite sports **magazine**.

magic (**mag** ic) a power that seems to make the impossible happen

Through his **magic,** he made the lady disappear.

magnet (**mag** net) a piece of metal that attracts things made of iron or steel

I wonder why a **magnet** is sometimes shaped like a horseshoe.

magnificent (mag **nif** i cent) great, glorious

The view down into the Grand Canyon was just **magnificent**!

magnify (**mag** ni fy) to make bigger or enlarge for easy viewing

We used a microscope to **magnify** the butterfly's wing to fifty times its true size.

maid a female housekeeper, a servant

The rich lady hired a **maid** to dust the furniture, vacuum the rugs, and polish the silver.

mail letters or packages that come through the postal system

Did you get any **mail** from your English pen pal?

main most important, chief

The **main** street in our town is called Main Street.

majority (ma **jor** i ty) more than half

The **majority** of the kids in our class elected Sheila class president.

make 1. to build, to create

I'd like to **make** a Mother's Day card instead of buying one.

2. to force

She will **make** me go to my room if I misbehave.

3. to cause

If you go on that ride right after lunch, it will **make** you feel sick.

male a boy or a man

There were five girls in the play, but there was only one part for a **male**.

mall an area of shops

The **mall** in our town has stores, restaurants, and a theater.

man a male grown-up

A **man** usually has to shave once a day.

mane long hair in the neck area of a horse or other animal

The horse's **mane** was a beautiful golden brown.

manage (**man** age) to direct an activity, to lead

Sometimes my father helps the coach **manage** our team.

mansion (**man** sion) a very large and expensive house

The **mansion** was so large that it looked like a hotel, but only one family lived there.

manufacture (man u **fac** ture) to make or produce a large amount of something

An automobile factory is a place where people **manufacture** cars.

many (**man** y) a large number

A very popular girl is one who has **many** friends.

map a drawing or chart of a place

The teacher asked me to point to Florida on the **map** of the United States.

marble (**mar** ble) 1. a hard stone used to make buildings and statues

> **Marble** is dug out of the ground, then cut and polished to bring out its beauty.

2. a small glass ball used in games

> He stopped the game of Chinese checkers until he picked up the **marble** that had rolled off the playing board.

1. march to walk in time with others, to parade

Our school band was invited to **march** down Main Street on Thanksgiving Day.

2. March the third month of the year

When **March** arrives, we'll go fly our kites; and if it's windy, they'll fly to great heights.

margin (**mar** gin) the blank border on a written page

When she corrected my paper, the teacher wrote a short note in the **margin**.

marionette (mar i o **nette**) a puppet moved by strings

The puppeteer closed the curtains while he fixed the **marionette**.

mark 1. a stain, a dirty spot

When its ink leaked, my ballpoint pen left a **mark** on my desk.

2. a grade, a rating

The "A" on my math test was the best **mark** in the class.

market (**mar** ket) a place where things are bought and sold

Every Sunday the farmers set up a **market** in the square.

marry (**mar** ry) to become husband and wife

She and her boyfriend agreed to **marry** and start a home together.

Mars the fourth planet from the Sun

Mars is the planet that is known for its red color.

marvelous (**mar** vel ous) wonderful, great

We had a **marvelous** time fishing and swimming off my uncle's boat.

mask a covering for the face

The catcher's **mask** protects him from being hit by the bat and the ball.

masquerade (**mas** que rade) a party where people wear costumes and masks

Three of us came to the **masquerade** wearing Batman disguises.

mat 1. a small rug

Mother asks us to wipe our feet on a **mat** by the front door.

2. a pad on the gym floor

The wrestling team always practices on a **mat** so people won't get hurt when they fall.

match 1. a contest

The wrestling **match** was over when he pinned his opponent to the mat.

2. a good combination

The blue shirt and slacks were a perfect **match**.

3. a stick that makes fire

He lit the **match** and threw it on the twigs, and we had a roaring campfire.

May the fifth month of the year

We always celebrate Memorial Day over the very last weekend in **May**.

maybe (**may** be) perhaps, possibly

I can't invite you over today, but **maybe** you can come tomorrow.

mayor (**may** or) the person at the head of a city government

The **mayor** promised that he'd make our fire department, police department, and school system the best.

meal the food eaten at one of three regular times of the day

Dinner is the one **meal** that everyone in my family eats together.

mean unkind, cruel

Hiding her eyeglasses was a **mean** trick to play on Alexandra.

meaning (**mean** ing) explanation, definition

I had to look up the **meaning** of that word in a dictionary.

measure (**meas** ure) to find the size of

We had to **measure** my bed before we could order a new cover that would fit it.

mechanic (me **chan** ic) someone good at fixing things, a repairman

He always loved cars, and he got a good job as an auto **mechanic**.

medal (**med** al) a badge given as an award

He was given a **medal** for bravery during the war.

medicine (**med** i cine) something taken to treat sickness or pain

The doctor gave me **medicine** that would bring my temperature down to normal.

meet to come together, to gather

Our club is going to **meet** once a week at my house.

melt to change from solid to liquid, to thaw

If the sun comes out today, all of that snow will **melt**.

member (**mem** ber) someone or something belonging to a group

Every new **member** of the team gets a uniform.

memorize (**mem** o rize) to learn by heart

We had to **memorize** our parts in the play quickly, because opening night was just one week away.

mend to put back in good condition, to repair

It took a big patch to **mend** my jeans because they were so badly torn.

menu (**men** u) a list of foods served in a restaurant

Whenever I get a **menu,** I look at the dessert list first.

message (**mes** sage) words sent from one person to another

I left a **message** on his telephone-answering machine.

messenger (**mes** sen ger) someone who delivers things by hand

The **messenger** took messages and packages from place to place on a bicycle.

messy (**mes** sy) sloppy, untidy

I know my desk looks **messy,** but I know where everything is on it.

microphone (**mi** cro phone) a small machine that uses electricity to make sounds louder

No one in the back of the room could hear the speaker without his **microphone.**

microscope (**mi** cro scope) a tool that can help us see tiny things by making then look larger

Through the **microscope,** we saw every little vein in the leaf.

137

middle (**mid** dle) the halfway point, the center

The double line painted down the **middle** of the highway divided it into two equal lanes.

midget (**mid** get) a person who is much smaller than normal

My friend Neil's father is a **midget,** but Neil and his brother are average height.

mild calm, gentle

The weather was **mild,** so we were able to go out on the boat.

minute (**min** ute) sixty seconds

There are sixty seconds in a minute and sixty minutes in an hour.

miracle (**mir** a cle) a wonderful happening that seems impossible

It was a **miracle** that so many of the passengers were still alive after that plane crash.

mirror (**mir** ror) a special glass that you can see yourself in

The wicked queen looked in the **mirror** and saw that she was no longer the fairest of them all.

miser (**mi** ser) a stingy person who hates to spend any of his money

Steven called me a **miser** when he saw me deposit my whole allowance in the bank.

miss 1. to fail to do something

When you **miss** hitting the ball in a baseball game, it's called a strike.

2. to feel sad about the absence of someone or something

I really **miss** my dog whenever we have to leave him in a kennel.

mistake (mis **take**) an error

If the TV is on while I'm doing my homework, I make one **mistake** after another.

mitt a kind of glove

I used a **mitt** today as catcher, and my mother used a different kind of **mitt** to take the hot pan out of the oven.

mitten (**mit** ten) a glove with one section for the thumb and another section for all the other fingers

My fingers seem to stay warmer when they're all together in a **mitten** than when I wear a glove.

mix to combine, to blend

When we ran out of green paint, we just had to **mix** blue and yellow paint to match the color.

model (**mo** del) 1. a small copy of something larger

I put together a **model** of the Concorde jet.

2. someone whose work is to pose for pictures

Our neighbor's son is a **model** who appears in ads for children's clothing.

modern (**mod** ern) up-to-date, new

My parents just bought a more **modern** refrigerator with an automatic icemaker on the door.

moist wet, damp

We used a **moist** sponge to seal and stamp all the party invitations.

money (**mon** ey) the coins and paper that we use to buy things, cash

At the end of our vacation, my father cashed all the Canadian **money** back into American dollars.

monitor (**mon** i tor) a student who helps with an easy job in school

Each week our teacher chose a different **monitor** to clean the board erasers.

monkey (**mon** key) a kind of animal with long arms and tail that help it to swing among trees

The **monkey** almost looked human as we watched him eating a banana and scratching his head.

monster (**mon** ster) an imaginary scary animal or person, an ogre

Jack met the **monster** at the top of the beanstalk.

month one of twelve parts of the year

My birthday is in April, the fourth **month** of the year.

mood the way you feel at a certain time

My **mood** is never good when I first wake up in the morning, but after breakfast I feel better.

moon the closest heavenly body to Earth, which it revolves around

Moonlight is really sunlight shining on the **moon** and bouncing back to us on Earth.

more a larger number of, the opposite of less

When the waiter brought the vegetables, I asked for **more** potatoes and less squash.

morning (**morn** ing) the part of the day before noon

I usually get up around six o'clock in the **morning,** when the sun comes up.

most the greatest in number

Everyone in the class sold plenty of candy bars, but Jenny sold the **most**.

motel (mo **tel**) a hotel specially for people who drive up in cars

On our car trip across the country, we stayed in a different **motel** every night.

mother (**moth** er) a woman who has a child or children

My **mother** had two babies, and I was one of them.

motorcycle (**mo** tor cy cle) a heavy bike run by a motor

Even as a passenger on his **motorcycle,** I had to wear a helmet.

mound a small hill

The pitcher stands on a small **mound** when he throws the ball.

mount to climb up

You **mount** a horse by putting one foot in a stirrup and lifting yourself into the saddle.

mountain (**moun** tain) a towering hill that rises high above the surrounding land

Skiers love to zoom down a steep **mountain.**

mouth the part of the face through which we eat, speak, and breathe

After the dentist give me an injection, my **mouth** was numb for hours.

move to change the location of

Please **move** your bookbag out of the aisle.

movie (**mov** ie) a motion picture, a film

The Wizard of Oz is a **movie** that features scenes in both black-and-white and color.

mud soft wet earth

Pigs love to roll in **mud** to keep cool.

1. mug to rob

The kids in that gang will **mug** any stranger who walks through their neighborhood.

2. mug a large, heavy cup or glass

Harvey always drinks tea from a **mug**.

murder (**mur** der) a killing, a slaying

The gangster used a gun to **murder** the man who had identified him to the police.

muscle (**mus** cle) a part of the body under the skin that makes other parts of the body move

Every **muscle** in my body was used during my exercise class.

museum (mu **se** um) a place that keeps and displays interesting collections for the public

Sometimes a children's **museum** will set up exhibits that can be touched by the visitors.

music (**mu** sic) pretty sounds that come from combining different notes

The **music** of the Beatles was the rage of the sixties.

mustache (**mus** tache) the hair above a man's lip

I pasted on a **mustache** when I played the part of a pirate.

mystery (**mys** te ry) a story about a crime that needs to be solved

A **mystery** written by Agatha Christie is always thrilling and scary.

myth a kind of story that shows the beliefs of a group of people

The ancient Greeks thought greed was bad, as we see in the **myth** of King Midas.

Nn

nail 1. a thin pointed piece of metal used to fasten things
> If they don't use a big **nail** to hold up this heavy picture, it will fall off the wall.

2. the hard part at the end of the finger or toe
> The champion women's runner liked to paint each **nail** a different color.

naked (**na** ked) completely undressed, nude
> You have to be **naked** before you get into the bath.

name the word by which every person or thing is known
> The teacher calls the **name** of each student when she takes attendance.

nap to sleep for a short time, to doze
> Grandpa likes to **nap** in the big armchair for an hour after lunch.

napkin (**nap** kin) the small square piece of paper or cloth used to keep clean at mealtimes
> We all need more than one **napkin** to wipe our hands and faces when we eat fried chicken.

nasty (**nas** ty) unpleasant, mean
> Only a **nasty** child would pull pranks on that nice old man.

nation (**na** tion) a place where people live under one government

Every **nation** has a flag with its own colors and symbols.

navy (**na** vy) armed forces at sea

A **navy** has ships and sailors just as an army has tanks and soldiers.

near close to, not far from

I live **near** the school, so I can walk, but Keith has to use the bus.

nearly (**near** ly) almost

He **nearly** lost a finger when he put his hand close to the electric saw.

neat well-kept, tidy

My sister keeps her room so **neat,** but mine is kind of sloppy.

necessary (**nec** es sar y) needed, important

In science class, we learned that fuel and air are **necessary** for a fire to burn.

need to require

The weatherman said we'll **need** our umbrellas because it's going to rain today.

needle (**nee** dle) 1. a small thin pointed tool for sewing

> She had trouble threading the **needle** because it had such a small eye.

2. a small tube with a pointed tip that is used for giving injections

> I knew I was going to get a shot when the nurse handed the doctor a **needle**.

neighbor (**neigh** bor) someone who lives nearby

> Our **neighbor** across the road came over to help Dad.

neighborhood (**neigh** bor hood) one particular section of a city or town

> All the kids in our **neighborhood** go to the same elementary school.

nervous (**nerv** ous) upset, tense

> I was so **nervous** taking that test that I forgot to put my name on the paper.

nest the home birds build for themselves

> The mother bird used twigs and grass to make a **nest** in a tree right outside my window.

net a fabric made of knotted rope with many regular holes in it, used to catch things or in certain games

> He slammed the volleyball so hard over the **net** that no one on the other side could return the ball.

new fresh, up-to-date

> We always get **new** clothes for the **new** school year.

147

news a report about something that just happened

We listen to the **news** twice a day so we can hear about all the latest events.

newspaper (**news** pa per) a printed report of events that is published regularly

I read the comics in the **newspaper** first, Dad takes the sports section, and Mom looks for the business section.

nickname (**nick** name) a cute, friendly name for someone

If you saw my friend Bob, you'd know why his **nickname** is "Red."

night the hours of darkness after sunset

I usually get about nine hours of sleep every **night**.

nightmare (**night** mare) a bad dream

Sometimes you wake up during a scary **nightmare**.

noise a loud, harsh sound

My parents said the party could be in our house if we promise to keep the **noise** down.

nominate (**nom** i nate) to name as a candidate for some office

I was really hoping that someone would **nominate** me for class president.

nonsense (**non** sense) foolishness

When my nine-month old brother talks, it sounds like **nonsense**.

normal (**nor** mal) usual, average

The doctor said my eyesight was **normal** and I wouldn't need glasses.

nose the part of the face through which we breathe and smell

I can hardly breathe through my **nose** during hay-fever season.

nosy (**nos** y) interested in other people's business, overly curious

My sister said that I was **nosy** for listening in on her telephone conversation.

note 1. a message, a memo

I wrote my grandmother a **note** thanking her for my birthday present.

2. a musical sound

When she sang that high **note,** the audience cheered.

notice (**no** tice) to see, to be aware of

Did you **notice** if I was carrying an umbrella when I left the house?

November (No **vem** ber) the eleventh month of the year

In **November,** Mom makes us a Thanksgiving dinner — roast turkey and stuffing — it's always a winner!

now at this time, at once

You have to let me know **now** if you want me to get you a ticket, because later they'll all be gone.

nuisance (**nui** sance) an annoying person or thing
When my little brother keeps asking to come along, he is really a **nuisance**!

nurse someone who is trained to take care of sick people
The **nurse** weighed and measured my baby brother.

Oo

obey (o **bey**) to do as you are told
The dog walker got all six dogs to **obey** her command to sit.

obnoxious (ob **nox** ious) annoying, disagreeable
The **obnoxious** child teased the little baby.

occupation (oc cu **pa** tion) the job a person does to earn a living
My aunt Sally changed her **occupation** from teacher to writer.

ocean (o cean) the large body of saltwater that covers most of Earth
I like to dive into the waves of the **ocean** and then lie on the sandy beach.

October (Oc **to** ber) the tenth month of the year
Halloween masks are sold all over town;
this year in **October** I'll go as a clown.

octopus (**oc** to pus) a sea animal with eight arms
We all thought that the **octopus** was the most interesting attraction at the aquarium.

odor (**o** dor) a smell, an aroma
A frightened skunk will spray you with a terrible **odor**.

office (**of** fice) 1. a workplace

> Two new typewriters were delivered to the principal's **office**.

2. a position

> When he lost the election for class president, he said he would never run for **office** again.

often (**of** ten) time after time, frequently

Do you write to your pen pal in England as **often** as twice a week?

open (**o** pen) not closed or shut

We walked all around the locked building until we finally found an **open** door.

operate (**op** er ate) 1. to work, to handle

> My brother knows how to **operate** a car with a stick shift.

2. to perform surgery

> The vet was scheduled to **operate** on our dog first thing in the morning.

opinion (o **pin** ion) a thought about something, a belief

My **opinion** of our substitute teacher is that she is better than our regular one.

opportunity (op por **tu** nity) a good chance to do something

We moved here when Dad was given the **opportunity** to change to a better job.

opposite (**op** po site) 1. on the other side of

The post office was across the street, just **opposite** our house.

2. completely different from

Harry is short with black curly hair, but his brother is just the **opposite** type — tall and blond.

orchestra (**or** ches tra) 1. a group of musicians who play together

The **orchestra** is made up of string, woodwind, brass, and percussion instruments.

2. the seating on the main floor of a theater

We were lucky to have seats in the **orchestra** section, because they were close to the stage.

order (**or** der) 1. to command, to direct

When recess ended, the monitor had to **order** the girls to stop jumping rope.

2. to ask for something to be delivered

Call Mario's and **order** a large pizza with sausage.

ordinary (**or** di nar y) usual, not special

We tried to buy Dad a unique watch for his birthday, but all the watches we saw were just **ordinary**.

organization (or gan i **za** tion) a group of people who work together for a special purpose

My aunt runs an **organization** that takes care of homeless people.

Oriental (Or i **en** tal) from the Far East

There are two **Oriental** boys in our class, one from Japan and one from China.

original (o **rig** i nal) 1. the first

This house was built for us, so we are the **original** owners.

2. new, fresh

Jim won the talent show because his unusual jokes were the funniest and most **original**.

orphan (**or** phan) a child without parents

Anne Shirley was an **orphan** who was adopted by the kind people of Green Gables.

outfit (**out** fit) a set of clothing or equipment

I bought a whole new **outfit** for skiing — jacket, cap, gloves, boots, poles, and skis.

oven (**ov** en) the inside of a stove, used for cooking

Doesn't the house smell great when there's a cake baking in the **oven**?

owe to have to pay

I **owe** him five dollars, but he said I could pay him back one dollar a week.

own to have to keep

I don't **own** a pair of ice skates, so I rent them at the rink.

Pp

pack to fill, to load
I tried to **pack** everything I'd need into one suitcase.

package (**pack** age) something put in a box or in wrapping paper
The postal clerk weighed the **package,** stamped it, and mailed it out.

pad 1. blank paper pages glued together at one end
We always keep a **pad** and a pencil near the telephone.
2. a cushion
Dad keeps a **pad** on the driver's seat for his bad back.

page one side of each piece of paper in a book
This **page** in the dictionary only has words that start with P.

pail a bucket
The baby used her shovel to fill the **pail** with sand.

pain an ache or soreness in some part of the body
I had so much **pain** in that tooth that I hardly noticed the shot the dentist gave me.

paint a liquid used for coloring or decorating
We used brushes to spread blue **paint** on every wall in the house.

pair two things that match
I thought I had put on a **pair** of blue socks, but out in the light I saw that one was brown.

pajamas (pa **ja** mas) a shirt-and-pants set worn for sleeping
During cold weather, I wear flannel **pajamas** to keep warm in bed.

palace (**pal** ace) a large beautiful home used by royalty
The Queen of England lives in Buckingham **Palace**.

parachute (**par** a chute) an umbrella-shaped cloth used to float safely through the air from an airplane to the ground
When his plane was shot down, the pilot was not afraid to jump, because he still had time to use his **parachute**.

parade (pa **rade**) a march in formation to celebrate some event
Santa Claus always appears at the end of a Thanksgiving Day **parade**.

paragraph (**par** a graph) a group of sentences on one subject
In the first **paragraph** of my report on Abe Lincoln, I just described his childhood.

parent (**par** ent) a mother or a father
The teacher asked to see at least one **parent** of each child during Open School Week.

park an area of land set aside for people's enjoyment
Our neighborhood **park** has a playground for children and some benches for adults.

part 1. a piece of the whole thing
Which **part** of the chicken do you like best, the leg or the breast?
2. a role in a play or a movie
Do you know who played the **part** of Dorothy in *The Wizard of Oz*?

partner (**part** ner) one of two or more people who are doing something together
Everyone had to choose a **partner** for square dancing.

party (**par** ty) a celebration
My cousin and I have the same birthday, so our family always has one **party** for us both.

passenger (**pas** sen ger) a rider on some kind of transportation
The bus was in an accident, but they got every **passenger** out safely.

paste something soft and sticky used to glue things together
We used a special **paste** of flour and water to make the papier-mâché animals.

pat to tap lightly with an open hand
When the dog did the trick I had taught him, I gave him a treat and a **pat** on the head.

patch a small piece of cloth sewn on to cover a hole

I needed a **patch** over each knee in my jeans.

path a track or trail for walking

The **path** through the woods was all muddy after the heavy rains.

patient (**pa** tient) someone who is being treated by a doctor

In the doctor's waiting room, the **patient** next to me was wearing a neck brace.

patriotic (pa tri **ot** ic) showing or feeling love for your country

The **patriotic** athlete saluted his country's flag when he won the Olympic event.

patrol (pa **trol**) to walk around an area to guard against trouble

The area that a police officer has to **patrol** every day is called his "beat."

pay to give money for something

I had to **pay** for the jacket with the money from my allowance.

peaceful (**peace** ful) quiet, calm

After the police broke up the fight, the block was **peaceful** again.

pedal (**ped** al) to use your feet to make something go

I could **pedal** my bike much faster if I wore sneakers instead of shoes.

peddler (**ped** dler) a person who sells things without a store

The **peddler** in the flea market was selling sweatshirts and T-shirts.

peek a quick sly look

I'll let you take a **peek** at one of your presents if you promise not to tell.

peel to remove the outer skin of

Uncle Ted has to **peel** a lot of potatoes when he wants to make mashed potatoes for everyone.

pen 1. a tool that writes with ink

A man in the park was using a **pen** to draw the trees.

2. a small fenced-in area where animals are kept

One of the pigs got out of the **pen** when someone left the gate open.

pencil (**pen** cil) a tool that writes with lead

I did my homework with a **pencil,** in case I had to erase something.

pen pal a friend you have through letter writing

Though we still have not met, I hope to visit my **pen pal** someday.

perfect (**per** fect) excellent in every way, without mistakes

I got a **perfect** score on the last two spelling tests.

perform (per **form**) to put on some act, to entertain

I'm always nervous when I have to **perform** a song in front of an audience.

permit (per **mit**) to allow, to let

If he promises to drive safely, my parents **permit** my brother to take the car out at night.

perspire (per **spire**) to sweat

We **perspire** when we get hot, and the moisture cools our skin.

pest someone or something that is annoying

My brother was bothering my friends and being a **pest** all afternoon.

pet 1. an animal that people care for

Before we got a dog, the only **pet** I'd ever had was a hamster.

2. a favorite person

The teacher's **pet** always gets the best jobs.

photograph (**pho** to graph) a picture taken with a camera, a snapshot

When my grandmother visits, she likes to see the old **photograph** of me as a baby.

piano (pi **an** o) a large musical instrument with eighty-eight black and white keys

I usually play the **piano** an hour a day to get ready for the recital.

pick to select, to choose

If you were old enough to vote, whom would you **pick** for President?

picnic (**pic** nic) a fun meal that you eat outside

We carried our **picnic** to the park in a basket.

picture (**pic** ture) a drawing or photograph

I took a **picture** of Ronnie in his cap and gown.

piece a part of the whole thing, a section

Please pass me a **piece** of the chocolate cake.

pier a landing place for boats, a dock

The cruise ship pulled away from the **pier** at exactly five o'clock.

pierce to puncture

Since Paula had the doctor **pierce** her ears, she wears little gold earrings to school every day.

pile a tidy or untidy stack

The **pile** of garbage in the empty lot grows bigger day by day.

pillow (**pil** low) a cushion that you rest your head on when you're sleeping

When I hit my brother with my **pillow,** the feathers went flying all around.

pilot (**pi** lot) someone who flies an aircraft

A few of us were invited to talk to the **pilot** about how he steers the plane.

pin to hold things together, to fasten

At the party, I was the only one to **pin** the tail on the donkey.

pinch to press between the thumb and fingers

My grandmother likes to **pinch** my cheek.

pipe 1. a tube through which liquids travel

That **pipe** carries water to our kitchen.

2. a device used for holding and smoking tobacco

Pictures of Sherlock Holmes always show him smoking a **pipe**.

pirate (**pi** rate) a person known for committing crimes at sea

The most famous **pirate** is Captain Hook from the story of Peter Pan.

pitcher (**pitch** er) 1. the player who throws the ball to the batter in a baseball game

Our best **pitcher** throws curve-balls the other team can never hit.

2. a container that holds and pours drinks

Mother filled a large **pitcher** with lemonade for the kids who came over to study.

plain 1. clear, simple

The directions were **plain,** so we had no trouble assembling the set.

2. not fancy

I wore a pair of jeans and a **plain** shirt to the party.

plan to decide how to do something

We'd better meet to **plan** that weekend trip.

planet (**plan** et) one of the nine heavenly bodies that orbit the sun

We live on the **planet** Earth.

plant to place in the ground something that will grow

Every student in the science class had a chance to **plant** some vegetable seeds.

plate a round, flat dish

Everyone had a large **plate** for his sandwich and a smaller **plate** for dessert.

play 1. to do something for fun

I need a lot of time to do my homework and a lot of time to **play** with friends.

2. to act out a part

There was only one part left for me to **play,** that of the seventh dwarf.

3. to make music

In my family, we **play** three different instruments.

pledge to promise, to swear
"I **pledge** allegiance to the flag of the United States of America and to the Republic for which it stands."

plenty (**plen** ty) a lot, a full supply
We had **plenty** of frankfurters at the cookout, but we ran short of burgers.

pocket (**pock** et) an extra piece of material sewn on to hold things
She had a **pocket** in her skirt, and she kept her keys in it.

poem (**po** em) a piece of writing that has rhythm and sometimes rhyme
This **poem** is a sentence that happens to rhyme;
but all poems don't rhyme, not all of the time.

point 1. a narrow, sharp tip
I like a fresh **point** on my pencil when I do my homework.
2. a score of one in a game
Each time you throw the basketball through the hoop from the foul line, you get a **point.**
3. a place
Can you tell from the map at which **point** we turn off this highway?

poison (**poi** son) something that can kill if swallowed
The exterminator came to put **poison** down for the roaches.

poke to stick with your finger, to jab
I had to **poke** the boy in front of me to keep the line moving.

police (po **lice**) a group whose job is to protect the people in their community

Extra **police** were on duty for the parade.

polish (**pol** ish) to shine something by rubbing

I promised to pay my sister to **polish** my shoes.

polite (po **lite**) well-mannered, courteous

Why should I be **polite** to someone who's so rude to me?

pony (**po** ny) a kind of small horse

A **pony** is little even after it has grown up.

poor needy, having little money

The **poor** people in our town can have free lunch at the church every day.

popular (**pop** u lar) well-liked, well-known

Popular movie stars have many fans.

portable (**port** a ble) able to be carried around easily

I put new batteries in my **portable** radio before I left for the beach.

portion (**por** tion) a part of something

Please wrap up the leftover **portion** in a doggie bag, and I'll take it home.

portrait (**por** trait) a posed picture of some person

There's a **portrait** of George Washington hanging in our school auditorium.

possible (**pos** si ble) able to happen
The weatherman says that snow is **possible** tomorrow.

poster (**post** er) a large paper sign or picture
The **poster** on that billboard can be seen from miles away.

post office (post **of** fice) a place where mail is handled
We went to the **post office** to buy a book of stamps and to send a Christmas package to Grandma.

postpone (post **pone**) to put off until later, to delay
We had to **postpone** our trip until the car was fixed.

powerful (**pow** er ful) strong
We need a **powerful** flashlight to use outdoors when we go on our camping trip.

practice (**prac** tice) to drill something over and over again until it is learned
If I start to **practice** on the piano every day, I'll be ready for the recital.

pray to speak to God
Do you think it's all right for me to **pray** for snow, or should I **pray** for more important things?

predict (pre **dict**) to tell what will happen
The *Farmer's Almanac* claims to **predict** the weather months beforehand.

prefer (pre **fer**) to like more

Would you **prefer** going ice-skating or seeing a movie?

prepare (pre **pare**) to get ready

I helped Mom shell the peas and **prepare** all the other vegetables for the stew.

present (**pres** ent) a gift

Why don't we all chip in and buy one big **present** for Mom's birthday?

president (**pres** i dent) the head of a government, group, or company

In the United States, we elect a new **President** every four years.

press 1. to put pressure on, to squeeze

Press harder if you want the tack to go into the wall.

2. to iron clothing

When our clothes get wrinkled, we have to **press** them.

pretend (pre **tend**) to make believe

I like to **pretend** that I'm sleeping, then scare my brother by suddenly opening my eyes.

pretty (**pret** ty) good-looking, attractive

There are many **pretty** girls in our class, but Wanda is really beautiful.

prevent (pre **vent**) to keep from happening, to block
We talked about how kids can help **prevent** a drought by not wasting water.

price the amount of money charged for something you buy, the cost
The first **price** of the sneakers was crossed out, and a new sale **price** was written in.

principal (**prin** ci pal) the head of a school
We always stop working when the **principal** of our school talks to us over the PA system.

prison (**pris** on) a place where criminals are kept, a jail
The judge sent the crack dealer away to a **prison.**

private (**pri** vate) 1. not open to the public
Frankie had to pay extra for me to spend the day in his **private** club.
2. personal, not to be shared by others
Now and then you need **private** time to sit quietly alone and think.

privilege (**priv** i lege) an extra-special right
When we fooled around in the water, we almost lost the **privilege** of swimming at that pool.

prize an award or reward for doing something best
At the fair, Mom won the **prize** for baking the tastiest cheesecake.

problem (**prob** lem) something that is difficult to solve
Trying to find seats for everyone was a definite **problem.**

program (**pro** gram) 1. a list of players and events
The usher gave each of us a **program** that told who the actors were and what songs they would sing.

2. a TV or radio show
I was out with my friends, so I videotaped the **program** to watch later.

project (**pro** ject) 1. a special activity
Justin and I built a model solar-heating system for our science **project**.

2. a public housing development
The **project** in our town was built for senior citizens and low-income families.

promise (**prom** ise) to guarantee you'll do something, to swear
If you **promise** to do something, you should do it.

proof the facts that show something is true
The police had **proof** that he was the killer.

property (**prop** er ty) 1. things owned by someone

When I go to camp, I put my name on all my **property**.

2. a piece of land owned by someone

The old man was a grouch who never let anyone step on his **property**.

protect (pro **tect**) to keep from harm

The police now wear bullet-proof vests to **protect** them from gunshots.

proud very pleased about something you or a loved one did

We were all so **proud** when my mother went back to college last year.

public (**pub** lic) for all the people, not private

If we go to the **public** beach, we won't have to pay.

puddle (**pud** dle) a small amount of water collected on the ground

After a heavy rain, there's always a big **puddle** at the bottom of the hill.

pull to drag something and make it move forward

I could hardly **pull** my sled back up that steep hill.

pump something used to push gas, air, or liquid from one place to another

Mr. Jennings always lets me use the **pump** at his gas station to fill my bicycle tires with air.

punch 1. a blow with the fist

The prizefighter was knocked out in the first round by a **punch** to the head.

2. a drink often made with fruit juices

The **punch** at Linda's party was great because they added raspberry sherbet.

punish (**pun** ish) to give someone the treatment he deserves for something he did wrong

My parents know that the best way to **punish** me for not coming home on time, is to not let me watch TV.

pupil (**pu** pil) a student

Sammy was the only **pupil** in our class who was not promoted.

puppet (**pup** pet) a kind of doll that we make move

The bear **puppet** fits my hand like a glove.

puppy (**pup** py) a young dog

A dog is a **puppy** until it is one year old.

push to shove something forward

We all had to **push** the car until it started again.

puzzle (**puz** zle) 1. a picture cut into small parts that you fit together

The first **puzzle** we bought for the baby had only four pieces and made a picture of an elephant.

2. a problem that you solve with pencil and paper

We have a crossword **puzzle** in our school newspaper every week.

Qq

quarrel (**quar** rel) to argue

We always **quarrel** over silly things, like who sits in the front seat of the car.

queen the female ruler of a country or the wife of a king

The **queen** wore a crown and sat on a throne.

queer weird, strange

We couldn't stop staring at his **queer** haircut.

question (**ques** tion) a sentence that asks for information

The speaker asked us to raise our hands if we had a **question** about his speech.

quickly (**quick** ly) fast, rapidly

We had to move **quickly** to get out before the doors closed.

quiet (**qui** et) without noise, silent

He wouldn't start the show until the chattering audience became absolutely **quiet**.

quit to end, to leave

He **quit** his job in September when he had to go back to school.

quiz a short test

She gave us an arithmetic **quiz** every day before she started the lesson.

quote to repeat the words of someone else

If you are going to **quote** the Gettysburg Address, make sure everyone knows that Lincoln said it first.

Rr

race   1. a contest of speed

The turtle surprised everyone when he won his **race** with the rabbit.

2. a group of people with a similar heritage

People of every **race** come to live here in the United States.

racket (**rack** et)   1. a kind of light bat with a net center used in games like tennis and badminton

I hit the ball with the wooden edge of my **racket,** so it never got over the net.

2. a noisy commotion

The neighbors' kids were making such a **racket** that I couldn't study and Mom had to speak to their parents.

radio (**ra** di o)   equipment that brings sound by electrical energy

We listen to news and music on the **radio**.

raft   1. a floating platform

At camp, we would have a race by swimming out to the **raft** and back again.

2. a kind of flat boat that you paddle

No one was allowed to ride on a **raft** unless he was wearing a life preserver.

rag a piece of old cloth

Dad gave me a soft **rag** to use in polishing the car.

railroad (**rail** road) a system of travel by train

We traveled all the way to Florida by **railroad** because Mom was afraid to fly.

rain drops of water that fall from the clouds

The weather forecast was wrong, and we all got caught in the **rain** without umbrellas.

rainbow (**rain** bow) an arc of colors that sometimes appears if the sun comes out after a rain

The first **rainbow** appeared when Noah stepped out of the ark after forty days of rain.

raise 1. to lift up

You'll have to **raise** your feet so that I can vacuum the rug under them.

2. to increase

If they **raise** the price of a movie ticket, I'll have to ask for a **raise** in my allowance.

3. to bring up and care for

She found her puppy at the pound and took him home to **raise** him.

4. to collect

We all sold candy bars to **raise** money for our school fund.

ramp a man-made slope used instead of stairs

They built a **ramp** in front of our school for kids who use wheelchairs.

ranch farmland used to raise cattle, sheep, horses, or other animals

Danny spent the summer on his uncle's **ranch,** where he rode horses every day.

rare 1. hard to find, scarce

One of the stamps in his collection was so **rare** that there were only two like it in the whole country.

2. cooked for only a short time, not well-done

Jason's burger was so **rare,** it was almost raw.

rash red, itchy spots on the skin

He knew from his **rash** that he must have caught chicken pox from Peggy.

raw uncooked

He took us to a Japanese restaurant, where we ordered **raw** fish.

razor (**ra** zor) a tool with a sharp edge that is used to shave hair

When the barber finishes cutting my hair, he uses an electric **razor** on the back of my neck.

reach 1. to stretch for something in order to get it

We put all the books on a low shelf so my younger sister could **reach** them.

2. to arrive at

How long does it take you to **reach** your summer home by car?

3. to get in touch with, to communicate with

I've been trying to **reach** him by telephone for the last two days.

read to look at and understand printed words

I **read** an amazing story about a college football player who broke every major scoring record in only three years.

ready (**read** y) prepared, set

If you dress in a hurry, you will be **ready** to go in ten minutes.

real true, genuine

Louis found a ring with a **real** diamond in it.

reason (**rea** son) an explanation, a cause

I need a note telling the **reason** for my absence yesterday.

receipt (re **ceipt**) a written note that shows something was received

She had kept her **receipt** so she could remember how much she'd paid for that sweater.

receive (re **ceive**) to get something that was given or sent to you

He did **receive** my letter, because I wrote the right address on it.

recipe (**rec** i pe) the directions for preparing some food

She had to buy bread crumbs for her fried-chicken **recipe**.

recite (re **cite**) to repeat something aloud from memory

My voice was shaky when I had to stand and **recite** the poem we had learned.

recognize (**rec** og nize) to remember someone or something that has changed or that you haven't seen for a time

I didn't **recognize** my first-grade teacher without her glasses.

reduce (re **duce**) to cut or lessen

I'm waiting for them to **reduce** the price of the game before I buy it.

referee (ref e **ree**) a judge in some sport

The **referee** got punched when he tried to separate the two boxers.

refreshments (re **fresh** ments) food and drink snacks

So many people showed up at the meeting that we ran out to get more popcorn and soda for **refreshments**.

refrigerator (re **frig** er a tor) an electrical cabinet that keeps foods and drinks cold

I put the milk back into the **refrigerator** to keep it cool and fresh.

refund (**re** fund) money paid and then returned

I'll try to get a **refund** for the six bottles of soda that we never opened.

refuse (re **fuse**) to say no to

I must **refuse** a second helping of chocolate pudding, because I am on a diet.

rehearse (re **hearse**) to practice for a performance
Could you hold this script while I **rehearse** my part?

relative (**rel** a tive) someone in the same family
Now Charles is my **relative,** because he married my sister.

remain (re **main**) to stay
We were told to **remain** outside the building until the fire drill
was over.

remember (re **mem** ber) to recall
Harvey is good at games where you have to **remember** facts
and trivia.

remove (re **move**) to take away
They needed a tow truck to **remove** the car that was smashed
up in the accident.

rent to lease
After the plane trip, we had to **rent** a car to get around Hawaii
for a few days.

repair (re **pair**) to fix
We were able to **repair** the old microwave oven so it was as
good as new.

repeat (re **peat**) to say or do something over again
At the end of the news show, they **repeat** the most important
stories.

report (re **port**) a story, a statement
There was a special news **report** after the air crash.

rescue (**res** cue) to save from something dangerous
We were able to watch the fire fighters **rescue** the little girl who fell down the well.

respect (re **spect**) to admire, to honor
We **respect** our flag, so we stand and salute it as it is carried by.

responsible (re **spon** si ble) 1. dependable, reliable
The teacher chose the most **responsible** kids to be monitors.

2. causing to happen
We were all kept after school until they found out who was **responsible** for writing the graffiti.

rest 1. a time to relax
The coach always gives us a five-minute **rest** between races.
2. the remainder
He took one bite of the candy bar, and I finished the **rest**.

restaurant (**res** tau rant) a place where people pay for meals that are served to them
Sunday is Mom's day off, so we eat out in a **restaurant**.

return (re **turn**) 1. to come back

> The cat wanders around outside, but I always know he will **return** when it gets dark.

> 2. to give back

> My books are two days overdue already, so I'd better **return** them to the library today.

review (re **view**) to go over again

I have to **review** all my notes before the test tomorrow.

revolve (re **volve**) to move in a path around something else

Did you know that it takes one year for Earth to **revolve** around the sun?

reward (re **ward**) the payment or prize for something special that you did

Jay got a **reward** for finding the lawyer's briefcase and returning it to him.

rhyme 1. words that end with the same sound

> *Funny* and *bunny* are a **rhyme**.

> 2. a poem

> "Jack and Jill" is a famous nursery **rhyme**.

rich having a lot of something, wealthy

Robin Hood stole from **rich** people to give to poor people.

riddle (**rid** dle) a tricky question with a surprising answer

Here's a **riddle** for you: When does December come before July? (Answer: in a dictionary like this one.)

ride to sit or stand while something moves you from place to place

It was fun to **ride** the monorail that took us around the whole park.

right correct

The college student on the quiz show won a car for giving the **right** answer to every question.

ring 1. a circle

Twenty people climbed out of a little car that drove around and around the center **ring** at the circus.

2. a piece of jewelry worn on a finger

Mom and Dad each wear a plain gold wedding **ring**.

3. the sound a bell makes

A **ring** of the bell signals the end of each round in a fight.

rink an area with a smooth surface for skating

Someone played the organ, and we zoomed around the **rink** to the music.

riot (**ri** ot) a noisy public brawl

When the kids started to push their way into the concert, it caused a **riot**.

ripe ready to be picked and eaten

We left the green berries on the branches and picked only the **ripe** red ones.

risk to take a chance where there is some danger

We were willing to **risk** going down that steep hill on the sled, because it looked like fun.

river (**riv** er) a long, flowing body of water with land on both sides

When the ice melted in spring, the water ran down the mountain into the **river**.

road a path or route used to travel on

There really is only one main **road** that goes through the center of our town and into the next.

roast to cook slowly in an oven

In the morning Mom baked the pies, and later she used the oven to **roast** the turkey.

rob to steal from

They were able to **rob** our neighbor's house even though the alarm system went off.

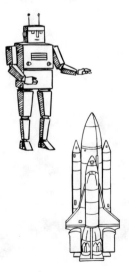

robot (**ro** bot) a machine made to do a person's job

Someday we may have a **robot** that looks like a person and can help us with all kinds of work.

rocket (**rock** et) a space vehicle that is pushed forward by gases coming out of the rear

The space shuttle rides to the sky piggyback on a big **rocket**.

rodeo (**ro** de o) a cowboy show of riding and roping skill

My dog is trying out for the **role** of Sandy in *Little Orphan Annie*.

The most exciting part of the **rodeo** was when the bronco busters rode the wild horses.

role a part in a play

My dog is trying out for the **role** of Sandy in *Little Orphan Annie*.

room a small part of a building set off by four walls

I have the smallest **room** in the house, but at least I don't have to share it with anybody.

rope many strings twisted together, a cord

We use lots of **rope** to tie the mattress to the roof of the car.

rotten (**rot** ten) spoiled, decayed

When we came back from our long vacation, we found that the tomatoes in the refrigerator had turned **rotten**.

rough 1. uneven, not smooth

We had to use sandpaper to smooth out the **rough** wood.

2. tough, crude

Some very **rough** kids were using our basketball court, so we didn't dare chase them.

rude having bad manners, impolite

I think it was **rude** of him not to answer our invitation.

rug a floor covering, a carpet

I tried to walk around the pretty **rug** because my sneakers were muddy.

ruin (**ru** in) to spoil, to destroy

He was very mean to **ruin** my sand castle by stepping on it.

rule a guide for how something must be done

There is a **rule** against bringing a camera into the museum.

ruler (**rul** er) 1. the person who runs a country

The **ruler** of a nation must always travel with bodyguards to protect him.

2. a stick that measures things

I used my **ruler** to draw a four-inch-square box.

run 1. to hurry, to race

It's late, but I can get to the store before it closes if I **run**.

2. to manage, to lead

Uncle Phil was hired to **run** the factory.

3. to operate

Do you know how to **run** the movie projector?

4. to flow

He pulled the stopper out of the tub to let the water **run** out.

5. to try out for an office, to campaign

Mom was happy to see a woman **run** for Vice President.

runaway (**run** a way) one who leaves home for good without permission

I would never be a **runaway,** because I know my parents love me.

runway (**run** way) a paved path used by airplanes for taking off and landing

> The jumbo jet moved faster and faster down the **runway** before it lifted into the air.

rush to hurry, to go fast

> Whenever I **rush** out of the house in the morning, I forget something.

Ss

sad feeling down, unhappy

He was **sad** to see homeless people sleeping on the streets.

safe protected, free from danger

The park is not a **safe** place to be after dark.

sail to travel across water

They were told to be on board at ten o'clock in the morning, because the ship was set to **sail** at noon.

salary (**sal** a ry) the pay a person gets for work, wages

Dad said it cost him a whole week's **salary** to buy the new TV set.

same just like, similar

Raymond and I laughed when we said the **same** thing at the **same** time.

sandwich (**sand** wich) food served between slices of bread

I traded my bologna **sandwich** for Arthur's ham-and-cheese.

satisfactory (sat is **fac** to ry) good enough

I got a **satisfactory** mark on my report, but my mother thought I could do better than that.

save 1. to put away for later use

> In our house, we all **save** our pennies in one big jar.

2. to rescue

> The fire fighters tried to **save** the people and their pets.

say to speak, to tell

> **Say** that you want us to go, and then we'll leave.

scale a machine that weighs people or things

> Mom gets on the **scale** every week but doesn't like any of us to see her weight.

scar the mark left after a cut has healed

> The **scar** on my right knee always reminds me of that bicycle accident.

scare to frighten, to startle

> We love to see monster movies that **scare** us.

scenery (**scen** er y) 1. the look of a place outdoors, the landscape

> When we drove to the country, my sister made a beautiful sketch of the **scenery** we saw.

2. the background on a stage

> We all helped to paint the **scenery** for our class play.

schedule (**sched** ule) a list of the times for things to happen

When we missed the nine o'clock train, we looked at a **schedule** to see when the next one would be leaving.

school the place where some people teach and others learn

Dad goes to **school** two nights a week to take a computer course.

score a count of points

The **score** is tied now, so they'll have to go into extra innings.

scramble (**scram** ble) to mix something up

If you **scramble** the letters in the word *leap,* you can get another word, *peal.*

scrape to rub or scratch something off

The painter tried to **scrape** some drops of paint off the windows.

scratch 1. to make a mark with something sharp

If you put your keys on the glass table, you'll **scratch** it.

2. to rub an itch

I'll feel better if you **scratch** my back.

scream to cry out, to yell

Some people heard her **scream** and came to help her.

screen 1. a framed piece of wire net, used in windows and doors, that keeps out insects

The **screen** in my bedroom window has a hole in it and lets in the flies.

2. a flat blank surface where pictures are shown

Ira has a tiny portable TV with just a two-inch **screen**.

scrub to rub hard while cleaning

Don't **scrub** the wall too hard, or you'll scrape all the paint off it.

sculpture (**sculp** ture) a work of art that is carved or shaped

That **sculpture** is of a running horse.

sea a large body of saltwater, the ocean

They were out in the **sea** during that hurricane, but they got back safely.

seal 1. a kind of furry animal that lives by the ocean

At feeding time, the keeper let the children throw fish to the **seal**.

2. the closing on something

The **seal** on a container of yogurt keeps people from opening it in the market.

search to hunt for something
The police had to **search** for the prisoners who escaped.

season (**sea** son) one of these four parts of the year: spring, summer, fall, and winter
In some parts of our country, there's not much change in the weather from one **season** to another.

seat something to sit on
There was no **seat** left for me on the bench, so I sat on the grass.

seat belt (**seat** belt) a strap that holds a person safely in a car seat or airplane seat
Dad never starts the car until I have my **seat belt** on.

secret (**se** cret) private, hidden
She locks her diary and hides the key in a **secret** place.

selfish (**self** ish) more interested in the self than in others
He bought a big tub of popcorn, but he was too **selfish** to share it with us.

sell to trade something for money
I can't buy a new bike unless I **sell** my old one.

send 1. to mail
Don't forget to **send** me a postcard from the hotel.
2. to order someone to go
The nurse said she would **send** me home from school if I didn't feel better.

separate (**sep** a rate) to split apart
When Mom got the wash ready, I helped her **separate** the light colors from the dark colors.

September (Sep **tem** ber) the ninth month of the year
Vacation is over, **September** is here;
school is open and autumn is near.

serious (**se** ri ous) 1. grim, not light and carefree
I knew something was wrong with Eric because he had such a **serious** look on his face.

2. important, major
We were having a discussion about **serious** books, like *Little Women*.

set 1. to put, to place
Set the plant down on the windowsill, where it will get sunlight.

2. to fix, to adjust
When we go fishing, we **set** the alarm clock to wake us at four in the morning.

settle (**set** tle) 1. to decide on something, to agree upon
Can you help us **settle** this argument about allowing girls on the team?

2. to locate, to make a home
My grandparents wanted to **settle** in Florida, where the weather is warm.

sew to work with a needle and thread

There's enough room left on my jean jacket to **sew** on one more patch.

shade 1. an area that is without direct sunlight

The big elm tree gives us **shade** in our backyard.

2. a piece of material that blocks the light

I pull my **shade** down before I go to sleep, so that the sun doesn't wake me in the morning.

shadow (**shad** ow) the dark outline of someone or something that is blocking the light

It was only my own **shadow** that scared me when I was walking home last night.

shake 1. to tremble without control

It was so cold waiting in that line that I started to **shake** all over.

2. to move a part of the body over and over

He had to **shake** his hands to get off all the water.

shape the form or outline of something

He could twist balloons into the **shape** of any animal.

share to divide and give a portion to someone else

Let's each have a burger and **share** an order of fries.

sharp 1. pointy

My handwriting is much clearer when I use a **sharp** pencil.

2. bright, clever

Wayne has such a **sharp** mind that he can beat anyone at chess.

shelf a flat board for holding things that is built on a wall or into furniture

Mom keeps all of our vitamins on a **shelf** right above the kitchen sink.

shelter (**shel** ter) protection, cover

When it suddenly started to rain at the beach, we found **shelter** under the boardwalk.

shine to look bright, to sparkle

Mom used so much wax to make the floor **shine** that it looked wet even when it was dry.

ship a large boat

Aunt Helen flew to Europe on a jet plane but came back across the ocean on a **ship**.

shoot to fire, to let fly

When you **shoot** an arrow, it whizzes through the air.

shop to go to buy something in a store

Saturday is the busiest time of the week to **shop** at the mall.

shout to call out in a loud voice, to yell

We have to **shout** to hear each other when a train passes.

shove to push

When the other boy started to **shove** Sam, a big fight broke out.

shovel (**shov** el) a tool used to clear snow or to dig with
> Three of us took turns using the **shovel** to move all the snow from in front of my house.

show to let see, to point out
> Next time you come over, I want to **show** you my new set of electric trains.

shrink to become smaller
> My sweatshirts **shrink** when I put them in the hot dryer.

shut to close
> We installed an automatic switch that can open and **shut** the garage door.

shy bashful around other people, timid
> He always looks down and acts **shy** when we meet other kids in the mall.

sick not feeling well, ill
> I was **sick** for two days when I had a virus.

sign to write your name in script on something
> Donald was able to go on the class trip when he got his parents to **sign** the permission slip.

silent (**si** lent) quiet
> The room was still and **silent** just before we all yelled, "SURPRISE!"

silly (**sil** ly) foolish

They all made such **silly** faces that I had to laugh when I tried to take their picture.

simple (**sim** ple) 1. clear, easy to understand

Addition and subtraction were **simple,** but now we're learning fractions.

2. plain

Some people lived in very **simple** houses, without even water or electricity.

sing to make music with your voice

After we salute the flag, we **sing** "The Star-Spangled Banner."

sink to go down deep into the water

They rescued the passengers and the crew before the ship started to **sink**.

siren (**si** ren) something that makes a shrill sound as a warning

The **siren** on the ambulance helps drivers ahead know it's coming.

sister (**sis** ter) a girl or a woman with the same parents as another person

My **sister** and I both have blue eyes, like our father.

skate to glide or slide smoothly along

I love to go roller skating, but I can't seem to keep my balance when I **skate** on ice.

ski to glide across the snow on special strips of wood
I learned to **ski** on a small hill, but now I take the lift up the mountain.

skinny (**skin** ny) very thin, slim
He was too **skinny** to be good at football, but we couldn't beat him in a race.

skyscraper (**sky** scrap er) a very tall building
From the top of the **skyscraper,** the hundreds of people below looked as small as ants.

slam 1. to close with great force
   Slam the door so I'll know you've gone out.
2. to hit with great force
   Did you see the car skid and then **slam** into the tree?

slap to hit with an open hand
Terry had to **slap** the dog on the back when he dirtied the carpet.

sled something you ride on over the snow
After a big snowstorm, we would zoom down the hill, one of us on each **sled**.

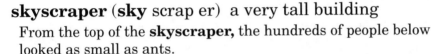

sleep to rest completely
Since Dad got his night job, he has to **sleep** in the afternoon.

slice to cut into pieces
Please **slice** my birthday cake so that everybody will get some.

slide to glide along smoothly

The closet door runs on a special track, so we can **slide** it open easily.

sling a support for an injured arm

As soon as the doctor placed my arm in a **sling,** I felt a lot less pain.

slip 1. to slide out of control

When she saw me **slip** on the wet floor, she grabbed my arm to stop me from falling.

2. to make a mistake

If you **slip** and mention Bert's surprise party to him, I'll be very angry.

sloppy (**slop** py) messy, untidy

The hardware store looked **sloppy** to me, but the owner knew where to find every nail and screw.

slow 1. not fast, sluggish

The ride uptown was **slow** because we were caught in heavy traffic.

2. not bright, dull

She was **slow** in reading and social studies, so she stayed after school for extra help.

smack to slap, to hit with an open hand

Katey gave Daisy a **smack** when Daisy tried to take Katey's doll away.

small little, not big

Marty is **small** compared to me, but he is my younger brother.

smart intelligent, bright

The baby was so **smart** that she knew all of her letters and numbers by the time she was three.

smash to break into many pieces, to shatter

I didn't see where the ball landed, but I heard it **smash** the window.

smell an odor, an aroma

Someone must have mowed the lawn, because there's a **smell** of fresh-cut grass.

smile to grin, to look happy

The photographer said something funny so that we'd all **smile** for the picture.

smooth even, not rough

The waters were so **smooth** that we didn't even know the ship was moving.

snack a bit of food eaten between meals

I have a **snack** of milk and cookies when I get home from school.

snapshot (**snap** shot) a photograph

I didn't know he was taking a **snapshot** of me biting into a big piece of my birthday cake.

sneak to creep, to act in a sly, dishonest way

He was caught trying to **sneak** into the movie theater without paying.

snow flakes of frozen water that fall from clouds
We will not be able to go to school tomorrow if we get ten inches of **snow** tonight.

soccer (**soc** cer) a sport played by two teams whose players may never touch the ball with their hands
Soccer is the only sport in our town where boys and girls play on the same team.

soft 1. not hard, flexible
When the snow is too **soft,** you just can't pack it into good snowballs.
2. not loud, hushed
My brother tunes the car radio to play loud rock music, but my parents tune it to play **soft** music when they take the wheel.

solve to find the answer to
I did the math problem three times before I could **solve** it.

son someone's child who is a boy
When Mom makes an appointment for me to see the doctor, she tells them she's bringing her **son**.

soon at a time that is almost here, shortly
Now that June is here, it will **soon** be time for camp again.

sore a cut or bruise on the body
It took a few days for the scab to fall off the **sore** on my knee.

sorry (**sor** ry)   1. apologetic

I said I was **sorry** about not inviting him, but Randy was still angry.

2. sad about

We all felt so **sorry** for the people who were left homeless after the earthquake.

sound a kind of noise

When we heard the **sound** of the smoke alarm, we ran into the kitchen to see what was burning.

souvenir (sou ve **nir**) something we keep to remember a special place, person, or event

A Mickey Mouse hat is the only **souvenir** I have from our trip to Disneyland.

speak to talk

My baby sister is learning to **speak,** so she can tell us what she wants now.

special (**spe** cial) unusual, not ordinary

Willie has to wear **special** eyeglasses that are unbreakable when he plays ball.

spectacular (spec **tac** u lar) magnificent, wonderful, offering much to see

We had a **spectacular** view from the top of the Statue of Liberty.

spend to use money for something

I'll **spend** my whole allowance at the fair this weekend.

spill to have what's in a container fall or run out accidentally

If you don't cover the thermos tight, the juice will **spill** out.

split to separate, to divide

His pants were so tight, they **split** when he bent over.

spoil 1. to ruin, to destroy

Do you think I'll **spoil** this picture if I make it smaller to fit the frame?

2. to go bad, to become rotten

If we're not home in half an hour, that container of milk in the backseat will **spoil**.

spooky (**spook** y) scary, weird

We sat around the campfire, telling **spooky** stories of ghosts and monsters.

sport a kind of game or physical activity

I like to watch the **sport** of tennis, but I really don't enjoy playing it.

spread 1. to unfold, to stretch out

Let's **spread** our blanket here, so that we won't have to walk back and forth on the hot sand.

2. to cover with a smooth layer

She **spread** peanut butter and jelly on all the white bread, and I closed the sandwiches and wrapped them.

spring the season of the year between winter and summer

  The birds fly south for the winter and fly back up north in the **spring**.

spy to watch secretly

  I may **spy** on him one day after school to find out where he works.

squash to crush, to mash

  Did he **squash** your sandwich when he accidentally sat on your book bag?

squeeze to press hard

  When you **squeeze** oranges, you get orange juice.

stable (**sta** ble) a building that houses horses

  When we returned from our riding lesson, we rode our horses back into the **stable**.

stack a tidy pile

  We carried a **stack** of magazines into the hospital for the patients to read.

stadium (**sta** di um) an athletic field with rows of seats for viewers

  Our city has a new all-weather **stadium** with a covered dome.

stage a raised platform in an auditorium or theater

  The set on the **stage** was built to look like someone's living room.

stamp 1. to pound the floor with your foot

In the parade, the marching-band members all **stamp** their feet in time to the music.

2. to put postage on mail

I forgot to **stamp** the letter to Patty, so it was returned to me.

stampede (stam **pede**) a sudden rush of people or animals

A couple of frightened cattle can start a **stampede** of the whole herd.

stand 1. to get up on your feet, to rise

We all had to **stand** to let the latecomers get to their seats.

2. to remain in one place

Let the cookies **stand** on the tray awhile until they're cool enough to eat.

3. to put up with

Can you **stand** the noise of the jet planes?

star 1. a point of light in the night sky

"Twinkle, twinkle, little **star**; how I wonder what you are . . ."

2. a shape with five or six points

A red **star** on our homework paper meant that it was perfect.

3. an outstanding athlete or actor

We knew that a famous **star** was in the limousine when we saw all the photographers.

206

stare to look at with wide eyes for a long time

I was so surprised to see Ivan that all I could do was stand and **stare** at him.

start to begin

The musicians didn't **start** to play until the leader raised his baton.

starve to be without food

The United States sends food packages to poor countries, where people would otherwise **starve**.

station (**sta** tion) 1. a regular stop on a bus or subway line

The closest bus **station** is four blocks from my house.

2. the number on your radio or TV dial

When Dad gets up in the morning, he switches the radio to a news **station**.

statue (**stat** ue) a carved figure of a person or thing

All the tourists had their picture taken in front of the **Statue** of Liberty.

stay to remain

Ask your mother if you can **stay** at my house tonight.

steal to take something without permission, to rob

I chain my bike up wherever I stop, so that no one can **steal** it.

steer to guide, to direct

I like the bumper cars because I can **steer** my car right into someone else's.

stiff not easily bent, hard

My new shoes were so **stiff** that I got blisters the first time I wore them.

stingy (**stin** gy) not willing to spend money, cheap

We wouldn't put his name on the card because he was too **stingy** to chip in for the present.

stink to smell bad

During the garbage collectors' strike, the trash left on the street started to **stink**.

stir to mix with a spoon

Wait until the marshmallows melt and then **stir** them into the hot chocolate.

stop to end, to cease, to halt

The taxi didn't **stop** at the red light, and that's what caused the crash.

store a shop, a market

A bakery is a **store** where cookies are sold.

storm very heavy winds with rain or snow

The **storm** lasted all through the night, and then the roads were flooded.

story (**sto** ry) an account of something that happened, a tale

My little brother likes me to read the **story** of the three bears over and over again.

stove a kind of machine used to heat food

Last night, Mom let me make popcorn on top of the **stove**.

strange 1. not known before

When the boy first came from China, our food was **strange** to him.

2. odd, weird

There was something **strange** about the man wearing sunglasses at night.

straw a thin tube used for drinking

Drinking soda can be messy unless you do it through a **straw**.

street a road or avenue in a city or town

We found a parking space on the **street,** so Dad didn't have to pay for a garage.

stretch to spread out, to make bigger

I needed a very large rubber band to **stretch** around all my books.

strict tough, stern

Ms. Hill is a very **strict** teacher who has lots of rules for us to follow.

strike 1. to hit, to smack

The boxer to **strike** first will take his opponent by surprise.

2. to stop work in order to get better conditions

If the bus drivers decide to **strike** for higher pay, my father will have to use his car to get to work.

strong healthy, hearty

I felt so weak with the flu, but after a week I was **strong** enough to go back to school.

stubborn (**stub** born) not willing to change

I tried to talk Laurie into joining us, but she was **stubborn** and wouldn't come along.

study (**stu** dy) to try to learn about something

This year in social studies class, we're going to **study** the countries and customs of North America.

stuff to fill up, to pack tightly

We were asked to **stuff** Christmas stockings with gifts for the children in the hospital.

stupid (**stu** pid) not smart, dull

I felt so **stupid** when she called on me and I didn't know the answer.

subject (**sub** ject) the topic, the issue

My vacation is the **subject** of my first composition for school.

subscription (sub **scrip** tion) an order to receive magazines or newspapers

To get that magazine for another year, I have to renew my **subscription.**

substitute (**sub** sti tute) to replace

I'm not a regular on the team, but they asked me to **substitute** for Tony when he broke his finger.

subway (**sub** way) an underground train system

We need special tokens in order to ride the **subway**.

successful (suc **cess** ful) having good results

The coach said that with a little more practice, we could have a **successful** team that would win many games.

sudden (**sud** den) unexpected

Our seat belts protected us when the car made a **sudden** stop.

suggestion (sug **ges** tion) a plan that you offer to someone else

They took my **suggestion** to print up raffle tickets to raise money for the team.

summer (**sum** mer) the season of the year between spring and fall

Cool lemonade is my favorite drink during the hot **summer**.

sun the star that gives us light and heat

Earth and all the other planets circle the **sun**.

supermarket (**su** per mar ket) a large self-service grocery

When Mom shops in the **supermarket,** she goes up and down every single aisle.

sure certain, positive

Check your test paper to be **sure** that you have answered every question.

surprise (sur **prise**) to come upon suddenly, to startle

Tom was able to **surprise** Sally with a party by having all the guests hide when she first came in.

surrender (sur **ren** der) to give up

When the enemy waves a white flag, it means they're ready to stop fighting and **surrender**.

swear to promise

In a courtroom, a witness must **swear** to tell the truth, the whole truth, and nothing but the truth.

sweep to use a broom to clean the floor

When I dropped the plant, I had to **sweep** up the wet soil.

swim to move through the water

The instructor taught me how to breathe correctly when I **swim**.

switch to change

Whenever I have a double of a baseball card, I try to **switch** it for one I don't have.

sword a long blade used as a weapon
Long ago, a knight had to know how to fight with a **sword** and shield.

syllable (**syl** la ble) a group of letters that make one sound
Syl is the first **syllable** in the word *syllable*.

symptom (**symp** tom) a feeling or condition that shows you are ill
Fever was the first **symptom** of David's flu.

synonym (**syn** o nym) a word that means the same as another
Glad is a **synonym** for *happy*.

system (**sys** tem) an organized way of doing something
I have a **system** of caring for my seven plants: I water each plant on a different day of the week.

Tt

talent (**tal** ent) an ability to do something well, a know-how

My mother has a beautiful voice and a **talent** for singing.

talk to speak

I really didn't hear the answer because everyone started to **talk** at once.

tame not wild, trained

We were able to pet the animals in the children's zoo because they were all **tame**.

tape 1. to wrap, to bind

Tape up that box so it will hold together when you mail it.

2. to record

Mom uses the VCR to **tape** her favorite soap opera while she is at work.

taxi (**tax** i) a car that you pay to ride in, a cab

The driver started the meter as soon as we got into the **taxi**.

teach to give someone a lesson, to instruct

He taught me how to ice skate, and I promised to **teach** him how to ride a skateboard.

team a group of people who do something together
We're getting a **team** of kids to work together and clean up that empty lot.

tear to pull apart, to rip
Did you **tear** your jeans when you fell off your bike?

tease to annoy, to pester
If you let your sister **tease** the cat, he'll scratch her.

telephone (**tel** e phone) a machine that carries sounds through wires
We have an answering machine that takes messages when we're not home to answer the **telephone**.

telescope (**tel** e scope) a tool that helps us to see things that are very far away
I looked through a **telescope** and identified many distant stars in the night sky.

television (**tel** e vi sion) a machine that uses electricity to bring us pictures with sounds
When our electricity returned after the storm, I turned on the **television** to see the end of the game.

temperature (**tem** per a ture) the amount of heat
The thermometer showed that the **temperature** of the water in the swimming pool was 78°.

temporary (**tem** po ra ry) lasting for only a little while

Calvin took a **temporary** job, because he had to return to college in September.

tent a cloth shelter held up by poles and rope

On my first overnight scouting trip, I set up a **tent** and slept in it.

terrible (**ter** ri ble) awful, horrible

The movie was **terrible,** the popcorn was awful, and the weather was horrible on the way home.

terrific (ter **ri** fic) great, wonderful

It was a **terrific** party and we all had a wonderful time.

test 1. to question, to quiz

The teacher will **test** us on the states and their capitals tomorrow.

2. to try, to sample

I'll **test** the temperature of the water before I dive in.

thankful (**thank** ful) grateful

The families in the burning building were **thankful** to the fire fighters for getting them out alive.

theater (**the** a ter) a place where movies or plays are shown

Our favorite **theater** has a wide stage for the actors and comfortable seats for the audience.

thermometer (ther **mom** e ter) a tool that tells the temperature

We found the **thermometer,** and Mom used it to see if I had a fever.

thief someone who steals, a robber

They finally caught the car **thief** near the mall parking lot.

thin skinny, slim

Tina is always eating pizza and ice cream, but she still stays **thin**.

think 1. to believe, suppose

I **think** there is a Santa Claus.

2. to use your mind to consider something

Who do you **think** is the better candidate for class president?

thirsty (**thirst** y) dry, needing a drink

I knew those salty potato chips would make me **thirsty**.

thoughtful (**thought** ful) concerned about others, considerate

It was very **thoughtful** of our neighbors to drop off the Sunday paper when we couldn't get out to buy it.

throw to fling through the air, to toss

Throw him a fastball, and you'll strike him out.

thunder (**thund** er) a loud noise caused by weather

It was a terrible storm, with **thunder,** lightning, and heavy rains.

ticket (**tick** et) 1. a pass that allows you to enter
> I showed my **ticket** to the usher, who led me to my seat.

2. a summons
> The time on the parking meter was up, and we found a **ticket** on our windshield.

tie 1. to fasten
> She knows how to **tie** her shoelace.

2. to even the score
> The teams were in a **tie** at the end of the ninth inning.

tiger (**ti** ger) a kind of large wild cat with stripes
The **tiger** paced back and forth in its cage while it waited to be fed.

tiny (**ti** ny) very little
We bought the baby little bootees for her **tiny** feet.

tired weary, exhausted
I was so **tired** after gym period that I almost fell asleep in my next class.

title (**ti** tle) the name of a book, song, movie, or play
The **title** of our national anthem is "The Star-Spangled Banner."

top the highest part
The ski lift took us all the way up to the **top** of the mountain.

tornado (tor **na** do) a strong wind that twists through the air

A violent **tornado** swept Dorothy's house right to the Land of Oz.

torture (**tor** ture) something that causes great pain

It was **torture** to wear shoes that were too small.

total (**to** tal) the whole amount

We collected a **total** of forty-three dollars for the March of Dimes.

touch to feel with your fingers, to make contact

If you **touch** the fence while the paint is still wet, you'll get paint on your hands.

tough 1. difficult, hard

The moving men had a **tough** time getting the wide sofa up the narrow stairs.

2. strong, sturdy

Our canvas tent was **tough** enough to keep us warm and dry during the rainstorm.

tour a trip around some place or places of interest

A guide met our class and gave us a **tour** of the new children's museum.

tourist (**tour** ist) someone who travels to see some place of interest

It was hard to help the **tourist** with directions, because he didn't speak English very well and we didn't speak his language.

tournament (**tour** na ment) a contest where several games must be played to find a winner

In the last Ping-Pong **tournament,** the other school won three games out of five.

tow to pull or drag along with a heavy rope or chain

They sent a truck to **tow** our car to the nearest gas station.

toy something that children play with

We bought a rubber **toy** that would float in the baby's bathtub.

trace to copy by following an outline

I started to **trace** a picture, but the art teacher wanted me to draw my own original work.

trade to swap, to exchange

Mom let me **trade** sweatshirts with Benny, even though mine was a gift from Grandma.

traffic (**traf** fic) the movement of people and different kinds of transportation

Around Christmastime, the **traffic** near the stores is always very heavy.

train a group of connected railroad cars

When the **train** jumped the tracks, the electricity was shut off until the problem was corrected.

trainer (**train** er) someone who teaches or drills people or animals

I saw them interview the **trainer** whose dog had been chosen to perform in the Broadway show.

transfer (**trans** fer) to move from one to another
When we moved in December, I had to **transfer** to a new
school in the middle of the term.

translate (**trans** late) to change into another
language
Jackie speaks Spanish, so she can **translate** for the new boy
from Puerto Rico.

transportation (trans por **ta** tion) a way of carrying
passengers from one place to another
Dogsleds are the only **transportation** in the far north.

trap to catch, to capture
The police were able to **trap** the wild dog and take it away.

travel (**trav** el) to go from one place to another
Dad spends two hours every morning just to **travel** to work.

treat 1. to pay for someone else
Mom is going to **treat** all my friends to lunch and a
movie for my birthday.
2. to take care of someone who is sick or
injured
We had a two-hour wait in the emergency room
before a doctor could **treat** my broken toe.

trick 1. a stunt done by a magician
His best **trick** that night was sawing the lady in
half.
2. a joke played on someone else
Perry played a **trick** of using a buzzer on everyone
he shook hands with.

trip to stumble

A crack in the sidewalk made her **trip** and fall.

trophy (**tro** phy) a prize given to a winner

Everyone who bowled on the winning team received a **trophy**.

trouble (**trou** ble) a difficult situation

Victor knew he was in **trouble** when the principal asked to see his mother.

true real, actual

The teacher told us to choose a nonfiction book, which is really a **true** story.

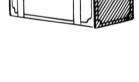

trunk 1. the thick main part of a tree

Carrie's dad slung the hammock from the **trunk** of one tree to the **trunk** of another.

2. a large storage box with a lock

My **trunk** had to be packed with clothes and sent to camp one week before I left.

3. the back of a car that is used to pack things in

When Dad wanted to carry the table home in the **trunk** of the car, he had to take out the two spare tires.

4. the part of an elephant's face that looks like a very long nose

The elephant took the peanuts in his **trunk** and put them into his mouth.

trust to believe in

Zachary is the treasurer of our club, and we **trust** him to take care of all our money.

try 1. to attempt

I'll **try** to fix the bike myself, but I'll take it back to the store if I can't.

2. to sample, to test

Why don't you **try** some of my frozen yogurt before you order your own?

tunnel (**tun** nel) a long hole or passageway dug underground or underwater

Sometimes people drive through a **tunnel** to get from one side of a river to the other.

turn 1. a spinning motion, a rotation

A **turn** of the top sets it spinning for almost a minute.

2. a change in direction or position

We missed the exit when we were driving, so we had to **turn** and go back.

3. a chance to take part in something

This week, it's my **turn** to walk the dog every morning.

turtle (**tur** tle) a kind of animal with a hard-shelled back that lives on land and/or in the water

A **turtle** pulls his head and legs into its shell when it feels threatened.

tutor (**tu** tor) someone who gives you extra help with a subject you're learning in school

When Susan was absent for a few weeks, her mother hired a **tutor** to help her keep up with the arithmetic lessons.

twin one of two children born to the same mother at the same time

Even though Jessica was Jennifer's **twin,** people thought she was a year younger.

twist 1. to wind

It was my job to **twist** the red ribbon and the green ribbon together to decorate the Christmas bulletin board.

2. to turn sharply and painfully

You can easily **twist** your ankle when you're learning how to ice skate.

Uu

ugly (**ug** ly) not pretty, unattractive

Alexandra is really very pretty, but she'll wear heavy makeup to play the part of the **ugly** stepmother in *Cinderella*.

umbrella (um **brel** la) a device we carry to keep us dry when it rains

The strong wind blew the **umbrella** inside out and tore the material off the spokes.

unbelievable (un be **liev** a ble) not to be thought true

His story sounded so **unbelievable,** but Walter said he was right there with him when it happened.

uncle (**un** cle) the brother of your mother or your father

Uncle Rudy is my favorite **uncle,** and I'm his favorite nephew.

uncomfortable (un **com** fort a ble) not easy or pleasant

My new shoes felt so **uncomfortable** that I couldn't wait to change into my sneakers.

understand (un der **stand**) to know what something means

If you don't **understand** the meaning of the words, look them up in the dictionary.

undress (un **dress**) to take off clothing

When I go shopping, I have to **undress** before I can try on new clothes.

unhappy (un **hap** py) not glad, sad

All the kids were very **unhappy** when they closed down the only roller rink we had in town.

uniform (**u** ni form) special clothing worn by every member of a particular group of people

I knew he was an American sailor just by the **uniform** he was wearing.

unlock (un **lock**) to open with a key

Dad had to **unlock** his briefcase to get what was inside.

unlucky (un **luck** y) having no good fortune

Mom thinks she's **unlucky**, because she never wins the lottery.

unpack (un **pack**) to unload

I had to **unpack** the whole suitcase because my bathing suit was at the bottom.

untie (un **tie**) to open

I had to **untie** the knot in my shoelace.

unusual (un **u** su al) not ordinary, different from others

The multicolored patches I bought to sew on my jeans should make them look very **unusual**.

useful (**use** ful) helpful, handy

My new book bag is really **useful,** because I can carry my books, my lunch, and even my sneakers in it.

usher (**ush** er) someone who leads you to your seat

The stadium was so dark that the **usher** used a flashlight to show us where to sit.

Vv

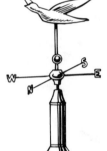

vacation (va **ca** tion) a break from work or school

We're getting out summer clothing and bathing suits for our Christmas **vacation** in Puerto Rico.

vane a tool that shows wind direction

The cold wind was coming from the north, so the weather **vane** was pointing to N.

variety (va **ri** e ty) a group of different kinds

There was such a large **variety** of flavors that I didn't know which ice cream to choose.

vegetable (**veg** e ta ble) a part of a plant that people eat

In science, we learned that the **vegetable** we eat is the root of the carrot plant.

ventriloquist (ven **tril** o quist) someone who can sound like his voice is somewhere else and look like he's not talking at all

The **ventriloquist** had a conversation with the dummy on his knee and even made us believe that they were singing together.

veterinarian (vet er i **nar** i an) a doctor for animals

We took the new puppy to the **veterinarian**, who gave him his shots.

vicious (**vi** cious) mean, ferocious

The dog's bark was so **vicious** that it kept us all from playing ball near that backyard.

victory (**vic** to ry) a triumph

After such a tough game, winning was a real **victory** for our team.

video (**vid** e o) able to be seen on a TV screen

Benjamin and I spent the whole afternoon playing **video** games at home.

view what you can see from one place

From one side of the plane there was a **view** of the tall buildings, and from the other side there was a **view** of the ocean.

visit (**vis** it) to stay for a while

Why don't you join us when my cousin comes to **visit** today?

voice the sound made by people

The coach used a bullhorn to make his **voice** louder out on the field.

volunteer (vol un **teer**) to offer to do something

We need someone to **volunteer** to make the punch for the party.

vote to make a choice, to select

We made up buttons that read: "**Vote** for Warren."

voyage (**voy** age) a long trip, a journey
Columbus set out on his **voyage** with three ships.

Ww

wagon (**wag** on) a four-wheeled cart that is used to carry things

My sister pulls all her dolls around in her little red **wagon**.

waiter (**wait** er) a man who serves food in a restaurant

The **waiter** went back to the kitchen to get me some ketchup for my potatoes.

wake to get up from a sleep

Did the baby's crying **wake** you this morning?

walk to move on foot

If the weather is nice, I'd rather **walk** to school than take the bus.

wall 1. a side of a building or a room

I covered one **wall** with posters of my favorite rock stars.

2. something solid that is built to divide two areas

In 1989, the Berlin **Wall** came down and the people from East Berlin and West Berlin were free to move back and forth between their two countries.

wallet (**wal** let) a small flat case used to carry money and papers

My **wallet** has two 1-dollar bills and a picture of my family in it.

want to desire, to wish for
I'm starting to keep a list of the things I really **want** for Christmas.

war a series of battles, a long fight
We have at least one special program a month to help in the **war** against drugs.

warning (**warn** ing) a notice of something bad that could happen
The first time the principal gave him a **warning,** but the next time he made him stay after school.

wash to clean with soap and water
Using a washcloth can help you **wash** dirt off your face.

waste to use carelessly, to throw away
If we didn't **waste** water all year, we might not have a shortage every summer.

watch 1. to look at, to observe
There were no seats left at the stadium for the big game, so we had to **watch** it on TV.
2. to guard, to protect
The security officer is paid to **watch** the store while everyone else goes out to get lunch.

weak not strong, frail
She had her meals on a tray in bed, because she was too **weak** to go to the kitchen table.

weapon (**wea** pon) anything used for fighting

G.I. Joe's **weapon** is a powerful gun.

wedding (**wed** ding) a marriage ceremony

It was a beautiful spring day, so the bride and groom held the **wedding** out in the garden.

week a period of seven days

Why do we have to go to school five days every **week** and be off only two?

weight how heavy something is

At the carnival, if the man couldn't guess your **weight,** you'd win a prize.

weird odd, spooky, creepy

We saw some pretty **weird** haircuts coming out of that barbershop.

welcome (**wel** come) to greet in a kind way

The teacher asked us to **welcome** the new boy and make him feel comfortable.

wet moist, not dry

Please take off your **wet** shoes and leave them outside until they dry.

whale a kind of large sea animal

A **whale** breathes air, has hair, and makes milk for its young.

wheel something round that rolls and makes things move

A screw was missing, so the front **wheel** of my bike started to wobble back and forth.

whisper (**whis** per) to speak in a very low voice

When she started to **whisper,** I knew that it must be a secret.

wife a woman who is married

When my uncle got married, his **wife** became my aunt.

wild 1. not tame

Wild animals are born free and should live free.

2. crazy, out of control

He was a **wild** kid who could never settle down to do his schoolwork.

win to do the best in a game or contest, to succeed

I try to be a good loser, but it's really more fun to **win**.

window (**win** dow) an opening in a wall that lets in light and air

The workmen had to cut the glass in my **window** to make room for the air conditioner.

windy (**wind** y) blowy, gusty

It was such a **windy** day that my hat blew off.

wing the part of a bird or a plane that helps it fly

The bird couldn't go south until its broken **wing** was healed.

winter (**win** ter) the season of the year between fall and spring

Now that I've learned how to ski, **winter** is my favorite time of year.

wire a long thin piece of metal through which electricity can travel

The electrical power travels through a **wire** and lights that lamp.

wish to hope and desire

Don't you **wish** you could be an astronaut on one of our spaceships?

witch a woman who is supposed to have magical powers

A bad **witch** gave Snow White a poison apple to eat.

witness (**wit** ness) someone who heard or saw something happen

The police asked the crowd at the scene if anyone had been a **witness** to the shooting.

wonder (**won** der) to want to know

I **wonder** why the moon seems to have different shapes.

wonderful (**won** der ful) great, spectacular

The fine weather and big waves added up to a **wonderful** time at the beach today.

work 1. to do a job

    I'd like to **work** in a bakery so I could eat all the chocolate brownies I want.

    2. to run, to operate

    We have a new VCR, but Dad is the only one who knows how to **work** it.

worry (**wor** ry) to be concerned, to be upset

You're right to **worry** about how we'll get to the game now that our car has broken down.

wrap to put a covering around

Would you place this gift in a box and **wrap** it for me?

wreck to damage badly, to ruin

Shelly didn't get hurt in the accident, but he did **wreck** the car.

wrestle (**wres** tle) to struggle with someone in a fight

My brother and I like to **wrestle** on the living room floor while watching the pros do it on TV.

writer (**writ** er) an author

Richard Scarry is a famous **writer** of children's books.

wrong not right, incorrect

The teacher took five points off for every **wrong** answer.

Xx

X ray (**X** ray) a special kind of picture, taken by doctors, of the inside of the body

When I fell off my bike, the doctor took an **X ray** of my arm to see if any bones were broken.

Yy

yard 1. a unit of length that is three feet or thirty-six inches

> He measured the big table with a ruler that was exactly a **yard** long.

2. a piece of land near a house

> Every Saturday morning, we meet for a game of touch football in the **yard** behind my house.

year a period of time that is twelve months long

> Once a **year,** every October, a photographer comes to take a picture of my class.

yell to shout, to scream

> We all stood up to **yell** cheers when our team came onto the field.

yogurt (**yo** gurt) a healthful kind of food made from milk

> I only like to eat **yogurt** if it has strawberries or bananas in it.

yo yo (**yo** yo) a round toy that rolls up and down a string

> I can roll the **yo yo** down, make it sleep for a few seconds, then pull it up again.

Zz

zebra (**ze** bra) an animal with black and white stripes, related to the horse

Its stripes help a **zebra** hide from other animals in the jungle.

zipper (**zip** per) a slide used to open and close clothing

If the **zipper** on my jacket gets caught, I just pull the jacket off over my head.

zoo a park where animals are kept

Instead of cages, our new **zoo** has large open areas where the lions and tigers can roam freely.